A Dragon,
a Dreamer,
and the Promise Giver

A Novel

A Dragon,
a Dreamer,
and the Promise Giver

A Novel

Joyce Strong

Destiny Image Fiction

An Imprint of

Destiny Image® Publishers, Inc.
P.O. Box 310
Shippensburg, PA 17257-0310

ISBN 0-7684-2182-9

For Worldwide Distribution
Printed in the U.S.A.

This book and all other Destiny Image, Revival Press, MercyPlace,
Fresh Bread, Destiny Image Fiction, and Treasure House books
are available at Christian bookstores and distributors worldwide.

For a U.S. bookstore nearest you, call **1-800-722-6774**.
For more information on foreign distributors, call **717-532-3040**.
Or reach us on the Internet:

www.destinyimage.com

THE FLOW OF SOLOMON'S LIFE

PREFACE

King Solomon reigned over Israel for forty years, from 960-920 B.C. Son of the legendary King David, Solomon was a vital link in the bloodline that would produce the prophesied Messiah, the deliverer of Israel.

This enigmatic king, however, who became a legend in his own right for his worldly wealth and human wisdom, was riddled with tragic flaws. As a spiritual leader, his behavior has mystified defenders of the faith for centuries.

A Dragon, a Dreamer, and the Promise Giver is a quest to find and define—beneath the trappings of power and politics—the battle for one man's heart. Rather than seeking to rewrite Scripture, this tale seeks to set the truth of what is in the Bible, along with what is revealed through history, within the context of probability.

I invite you to engage in the journey. Perhaps it will change your life.

PROLOGUE

A foul plot festered in the heart of Traeh, the ancient Dark Dragon. Across the vast expanse of time, the beast's cold stare penetrated the mist of earth's circumstances and sought an infant's sceptered hand.

"The divine promise over the child is great...and so must be his fall," Traeh growled as he spat out the pronouncement. After licking his lips, as though to taste again the bitter words, he strained to see the future more clearly. But all was shrouded in murky darkness.

The slithering, heaving sides of the loathsome beast twitched with excitement as he contemplated the challenge. "I will bide my time," hissed the creature. He writhed in forced restraint, a stench rising from the sod beneath his belly....

Far above and beyond the lurking Traeh, in the glory of the seventh Heaven, the divine Promise Giver measured the moves of the great dragon. He knew the reptile's patience. But His own was greater.

In the cosmic gulf between them, ponderous iron scales emerged, suspended between Heaven and earth, to weigh time to come. On one side, nestled in a gilded saucer hanging from massive links of chain, lay the child, Solomon. On the other side, in a matching saucer, and perfectly balancing the softly sleeping boy, lay a gift wrapped in blazing color. Crimson sparks shot from the second saucer and into the sky around it, as far as the eye could see.

In words that fell like sparkling crystal shards of light to the hell below, the Promise Giver spoke. *His life is Mine. You cannot have him*!

"Ah," hissed the Dark Dragon, his breath rising in noxious fumes toward the heavens, darkening the stars and poisoning planets on its way. "It's not his life I want; it's his heart!" The words slowly rose from deep within the evil of his soul, coming out in an eerie, hollow cackle.

Traeh studied the waiting heart of the infant—the future king of Israel—his own small heart filled with hatred and his yellow eyes squinting against the brilliant light of the Promise Giver's words, which still hung in the air....

PART I

THE STAGE IS SET

Chapter One

The Inheritance

The sheltered son of the mighty King David and Queen Bathsheba grew strong, nurtured by glorious tales of valor and dark lessons learned in sorrow. Throughout Solomon's childhood, Jehovah, the God of the seventh Heaven, invaded every moment of consequence. The promise propelled each event into significance.

As the child came of age, the future became today, and the boy felt the weight of all that lay ahead....

Solomon couldn't sleep. As the moon rose high in the night sky, the young, future monarch leaned out his window, palms down on the sill, head thrown back, lost in reflection. His languid, dark eyes searched the heavens for something secure, something comforting.

The day had been long and filled with exhilaration and wonder as he and his father had paced off the dimensions of the Dwelling for Jehovah that Solomon would someday build. Very clearly, the moment that loomed ahead—when he would take on his legendary father's mantle of kingship— was fast approaching, and the mere thought of it took his breath away. King of Israel, he mouthed silently, almost afraid to pronounce it aloud.

I am no warrior like Father, he continued in the solitude of his reflections, *although I will do what I must to defend myself when pressed*. His voice returning, "Philosopher, yes, with a poetic bent for the mystical...in that way I am like him," he ventured, "but no warrior." He had not been schooled in warfare in the desert as had his father; instead, he had been schooled in world philosophy, architecture, Jewish history, foreign languages, literature, and the arts—all in the comfort of the palace.

Politics

Straightening himself up after having leaned out of the window for some time, he stretched his arms to the ceiling and let out a big yawn.

"Or maybe just a tired diplomat!" he laughed a bit wearily. His best friend, Simeon, would attest to the diplomat part. He could always get others to settle their differences—while making each of them think they had won.

But facing national intrigue was another matter. The young heir had been but a small child when his much older brother, Absalom, had made his bid for the throne—and it had been gruesome business. David's pain had been immense when his commander, Joab, had subdued the rebellion by unmitigated and unnecessary murder. Even the vague memory of it sent chills down Solomon's spine.

A worried look moved onto the boy's face. Into the night he whispered, "There's still an older stepbrother—Adonijah—who undoubtedly eyes the throne and who uncannily fits every description I've heard about Absalom." Solomon tried to shake the shades of fear from his heart. His father's preferential love for him had always set him at odds with his siblings.

"Father will tell me what to do," he concluded, confident that dealing with this possible threat would be a simple task.

Solomon was no coward, but he secretly hated strife. Although few would believe it, in this too, the boy was like his father. "Thank God, there is peace in the land now," he said with relief, as he turned away from the window and contemplated sleep.

Deciding against sleep, he stepped back to the window, leaned out once more, and inhaled deeply of the night air. He sighed as he deftly brushed a straying strand of jet-black hair back into place with the palm of his right hand.

"If I can simply maintain the peace—negotiate well to save us unnecessary grief...But it'll take more wisdom than any man could come by naturally," he whispered in the direction of the sky. "And who will help me?" he quizzed the stars. "The two men I trust most besides Father are Nathan and Simeon—but one is getting old and will be gone soon, and the other is very young and knows no more than I!" He felt strangely alone.

Becoming increasingly restless, he turned to pace the length of his moonlit bedchamber, seeking to ease the tension, his mind racing. After what seemed like an hour, but was in reality only a few minutes, he came to a standstill in the center of the moonlit room. With hands on hips, chin jutting out in determination, and head cocked toward the open window, he searched the star-spangled sky beyond.

Tossing off the fear that nagged him, he whispered the phrase again to the stars, as though they could make it be: "If I can simply maintain the peace and negotiate well..." And then, singling out one particularly bright star, he addressed it in his most statesmanlike voice. "Well, everyone has his price, doesn't he?"

An icy voice responded soundlessly, *And you, Solomon? Do you have a price as well?*

At that, Solomon shook his head to drive the sinister presence from his mind. "You *really* need some sleep!" he admonished himself aloud, dismissing the foreboding shadow that flitted briefly around his heart.

The Sleepless Monarch

In another part of the gold and cedar-paneled palace, the old king—like his young son—could not sleep. While Solomon was lost in thoughts of peace, David was lost in dreams of worship.

That day had been one of the most significant in both their lives. The weight of the vision that had driven the king for decades—the vision of providing a permanent sanctuary for the God of Israel—had been transferred to his young son's shoulders. As king and son had paced off Mt. Moriah together from dawn until late afternoon—and pored over the detailed temple plans written on the yellowed, crinkled parchments long hidden in the king's desk for this day—the heart of rulership had informally passed from one to the other. There had been no bold proclamation, no trumpet blasts marking this day—only the passing of the spiritual scepter that was inextricably bound up in the worship of Jehovah.

What mattered more to David than willing the crown to his son was willing him his own love for Jehovah. The drama that had first played out in the heavens on a night like this one when he was a twelve-year-old watching his family's evening sacrifice—the one that had taken him deep into the heart of his God—still burned in his memory. The mystery in which it remained shrouded haunted him day after day—the mystery of the Messiah to come.

Through Very Different Eyes

As both the king and the king-to-be gazed out of their respective windows toward the south in the direction of Bethlehem, David's hometown, the blast of a trumpet split the sky. Sounding from somewhere beyond the stars in the distance, it ripped through the air, strangely fusing all the heavens into one glorious mural of victory somehow yet to come.

The vision has returned, David gasped. The aging king clutched the hand-carved frame of the window to steady himself.

From the east and from the west, pressing in upon their view from opposite directions, two enormous, rough-hewn beams—one vertical and one horizontal—forged their way across the sky, as if carried by some invisible giants. As they met, they shifted into place upon one another, forming a great "T" in the heavens.

Solomon, alarmed, furrowed his brow and wondered. *What could this mean? What portent of my future might the ponderous images carry?* He tensely searched the sky for meaning, small beads of perspiration appearing on his forehead.

As father and son stood transfixed at their windows, the vision played on. While the trumpet's call continued, a figure—not unlike that of one of the shepherds with whom David had kept company as a child—strode with purpose toward the crossed beams.

But as the simple, sandaled figure neared the beams, His image was transformed! In His place there stood a King—a regal King dressed in a flowing white linen robe gathered at the waist by a golden sash. On His head rested a crown of pure gold, studded with jewels of every color. *This I can understand*, breathed a momentarily relieved Solomon.

17

The face of the mystical King was weathered by warfare, yet soft with compassion; His bearing majestic, yet gentle and inviting.

As this heavenly King looked down at them both, David alone returned His gaze, his own heart pierced to the core by the love he saw in those eyes! In awe and with no hesitation, David pledged anew his allegiance to this King who had set his heart ablaze in the space of a single moment those many years ago. To Solomon, the scene remained a mystery.

Unexpected Turn

Then, as if by some strange compulsion, the King of the vision backed up against the crossed beams, spreading His arms to conform to the wood's design. As He pressed against the beams, He found Himself held fast to their rough surface.

What happened next sent shock waves through father and son. Evil of every kind, transformed into great leaden spears, flew at the captive monarch, piercing Him again and again!

As the very air surrounding the King shriveled up with the pain, His death began. The great love and agony that gripped the heavens gripped their souls as well, as they gazed upon the scene, appalled.

As the scene faded, another quickly took shape before their eyes. The glistening contour of a throne—the great size of which had never been seen on earth—emerged where the beams had stood just a moment before.

As David and Solomon both strained to see the mysterious King upon the mystical golden throne, sudden bursts of brilliant color shot forth, blinding them momentarily.

The Shepherd King

The vision continued, but the uncommon had become common. Father and son found themselves standing unnoticed in the street below their bedroom windows. This too was a vision David had seen before, and now his awestruck son witnessed it as well.

Crowds were gathering to the left just inside the city's main gate, and the air was charged with festivity.

"He's coming! The King is coming!" Men, women with babies in their arms, and children passed the news, all chattering at once, as they rushed toward the crowd that was growing rapidly. As they ran, they tore palm branches from the trees and waved them wildly in the air!

"Hosanna to the King! Blessed is He who comes in the name of the Lord!" the cries rang.

And then He appeared. Solomon expected to see the grandest monarch of all time being carried with pomp and circumstance through the gates. Instead, his jaw dropped in amazement at what emerged as the crowd split to let the King through.

A plain man in a simple, nondescript robe, gathered at the waist by a worn leather belt, rode astride a young donkey. His sandaled feet, dusty and callused from endless miles of travel on foot, hung nearly to the ground from the sides of the small animal. His face and hands were bronzed from the sun; His hair and beard framed His features in soft brown tones.

As He neared the spot where David and Solomon stood side by side and riveted to the ground, the King's eyes probed David's for an instant. But in that instant, the "knowing" of a twelve-year-old boy returned once again.

This was the same King who hung on the crossed beams and who sat upon the golden throne!

But Solomon's gaze was fixed elsewhere—on the crowd shouting and pouring adoration upon the Shepherd King. The adrenaline pumped through his body. *To be so adored! Will the world treat me this way as well when I am king?* he wondered in that split second.

The two men simultaneously found themselves back in their bedchambers, and the sky back to its former starry stillness as though nothing had happened. But both men knew otherwise. As each slipped into bed between silken sheets, he remained haunted by the images of only a few moments before.

In one room, an elderly monarch's heart began to stir with a familiar passion.

"Someday the King of kings will come—the Savior of the world!" he spoke aloud with certainty. "But will we know Him when He comes?" The thought of his own nation being unprepared...of missing the majesty wrapped in a shepherd's cloak...shook David to the core. Only that possibility could cause David to truly fear.

As he whispered his love to this King, hope settled peacefully upon his heart once again. He could face sleep tonight with nothing but sweet anticipation of the day every knee in Israel would bow to this eternal King.

Meanwhile, Solomon too fell asleep, but with his own dreams of *mortal* majesty—of power, palaces, and promises to fulfill.

In the heart of this precocious son of David, the future temple took clear and definite shape. He would surely build it, and it would be a most amazing structure—fit for the heavenly Presence it would invite. This edifice would be the envy of the rest of the world for generations to come. The beauty he imagined for it, both inside and out, was breathtaking not only in its richness of color and design, but also in its awe-inspiring grandeur.

However, shrouded in the shadows of his heart lurked one doubt: Would he ever comprehend the depth of his father's relationship with Jehovah? He marveled at it from afar. He saw the sense of it, but didn't *know* it.

Stone and mortar he understood. Elegant columns reaching to the sky—with these he felt at home. Symmetry and the intricacies of design fascinated him. But the passion that consumed his beloved father for the things of God—this remained a mystery to Solomon.

He would build this place of worship for his father, for their national identity, and for the love of beauty. It would be a joy for all to behold!

The tiniest shadow—a mere pinprick of darkness—a duality, if you will, slipped into the corridors of the boy's heart. Eyes trained intently, ears cocked to catch every nuance, the patient Traeh croaked with pleasure.

CHAPTER TWO

SECURING THE FUTURE

The next two years passed quietly. Solomon grew in confidence; David aged rapidly. While Nathan and Solomon knew David's intention to put Solomon on the throne, everyone else was in the dark; they awaited David's choice, afraid the king would die before establishing a successor.

In this vacuum, Adonijah built his strategy. He indeed had kingship on his mind. While Solomon and his renowned father were thinking of the future, Adonijah was making the most of the present. Just as had his late stepbrother Absalom before him, Adonijah was gathering admirers and playing the part of a monarch, minus the crown. Everywhere he went, chariots accompanied him; fifty runners preceded his entourage, assuring him a grand entrance. While David knew of his son's posturing, he characteristically did nothing.

Finally one day, Adonijah made his move. His grand procession traveled to the Stone of Zoheleth near EnRogel. There they ceremonially sacrificed sheep and cattle, as was the custom, in preparation to be pronounced king. Abiathar the priest poured anointing oil upon Adonijah's head; Joab, David's pragmatic army commander who forever misjudged David's intent, pledged his allegiance to Adonijah. A great party followed; all David's children were invited—save Solomon.

The Ruse Detected

Meanwhile, Nathan the prophet, David's friend and advisor of many years, discovered the plot and shared it with Bathsheba—who promptly told David. This bid for the throne forced David's hand. Ready or not, Solomon would have to be installed as king before Adonijah returned to Jerusalem to have himself declared king before all the people.

Hastily, David and Nathan took the young man to the springs at Gihon where, after their own sacrifices and prayers, Zadok the priest poured anointing oil upon Solomon's head. They hurried back to Jerusalem to call an assembly and proclaim Solomon king. This preemptive move threw Adonijah and his alliance into disarray; they scattered, fearing for their lives.

The threat dissolved and life went on. The whole affair, however, propelled the ailing David into serious preparation for his own death. First, the plans for the temple must be made public and help must be solicited. A proper coronation for Solomon would follow.

Providing for the Temple

During the ensuing months, Solomon watched in amazement as his father moved systematically and thoroughly—although at almost a fever pitch—to structure and establish the order of worship and work at the future temple. The 38,000 members of the tribe of Levi—designated by the patriarch Moses to exclusively serve in leading Israel in worship—were divided and assigned their duties. Unlike the detailed instructions regarding the temple itself, *these* instructions were uninspiring to Solomon. Gratefully he watched from afar as his father made assignments and clarified issue after issue regarding worship procedure and temple care.

On the momentous day that David explained to all the people God's plan to have Solomon build the temple, he also called them to personally give of their substance to make it a reality. How inspiring it was to see David's passion as he gave of his own personal treasures and wealth to the building of the house of God! Equally inspiring was the response of all the king's leaders. The air was charged with excitement as the leaders of families of the tribes of Israel, the commanders of the army, and all the king's officials gave generously to the work ahead. Gold, silver, and bronze coins and precious artifacts were piled high in the palace courtyard.

Before all the people, the king bowed in humble devotion to God and His enduring call on all their hearts. For all to hear, David praised the Lord, saying,

Praise be to You, O Lord,
God of our father Israel,
From everlasting to everlasting.
Yours, O Lord, is the greatness and the power
And the glory and the majesty and the splendor,
For everything in heaven and earth is Yours.
Yours, O Lord, is the kingdom;
You are exalted as head over all.
Wealth and honor come from You;
You are the ruler of all things.
In Your hands are strength and power
To exalt and give strength to all.
Now, our God, we give You thanks,
And praise Your glorious name.[1]

And then, as he and Solomon knelt side by side, David prayed from the depths of his heart. Softly, earnestly he

---

1. First Chronicles 29:10-13.

spoke: "I know, my God, that You test the heart and are pleased with integrity. All these things have I given willingly and with honest intent. And now I have seen with joy how willingly Your people who are here have given to You. O Lord, God of our fathers Abraham, Isaac, and Israel, keep this desire in the hearts of Your people forever, and keep their hearts loyal to You. And give my son Solomon the wholehearted devotion to keep Your commands, requirements, and decrees and to do everything to build the palatial structure for which I have provided."

Despite his frailty, David straightened himself up to his full height, and Solomon followed suit. With great dignity that rose from forty years of leading this great people in honor before the whole world, the king's voice fairly thundered, "Praise the Lord your God!" And as if joined at the heart with their beloved leader, all the assembly erupted in spontaneous praise to the Lord, the God of their fathers. Then as one, they bowed low and fell prostrate before the Lord and the king.

Tears flowed freely down David's wrinkled cheeks.

Final Preparations

Inch by inch, the reality of Solomon's kingship became known. The people had readily received David's call to support his son with all their hearts, and now it was time to make the coronation official. So a royal assembly was called. As Solomon knelt before the officials, Zadok the high priest once again anointed his head with oil. His kingship was now undisputed. All Israel celebrated with great joy in the presence of the Lord, and the feasting began.

Taking the Throne

Later that day, as Solomon was ushered down the corridors to the throne room of his father David, the palace shook with the cry, "Long live King Solomon. Long live the son of David!" Emotion surged within the new monarch. Though he fought to suppress them, tears streamed down his face.

As Solomon took the throne in the magnificent hall, his slightly stooped but still regal father bowed low before him, steadied by Nathan. Off to the side, in a place of honor, his mother, the forever radiant and devoted Bathsheba, bowed as well. She had waited for this moment ever since her son was born.

Solomon could barely comprehend what had just transpired, even though he had dreamed of it since childhood. And then, like a hit to his chest that knocked the wind out of him, he was struck by his seemingly indomitable parents' mortality.

Probing Reflections

What will life be like without them? The thought was entirely new. *Have I learned well all I need to know?* In a split second, the lessons he received at his father's knees flashed through his mind.

One day's conversation in particular burned in his memory. It had been a soft, summer day, and his father had been unusually reflective. They had been reclining in the garden on the palace rooftop. The sun had glinted through David's hair, giving the slightly graying brown curls a golden touch. Solomon had been only five years old.

In a faraway voice—at times intense, at times tinged with sorrow—his gentle father spoke words that had perplexed the little boy.

Above all else, guard your heart,
for it is the wellspring of life.
Let your eyes look straight ahead,
fix your gaze directly before you.
Make level paths for your feet
and take only ways that are firm.
Do not swerve to the right or the left;
keep your foot from evil.[2]

It wasn't the only time his father had stressed this to him. The young king hoped he would understand its implications when he needed them. Perhaps he would remember to tell this to his own son someday....

His reverie was broken by a palace guard's booming voice.

"My liege, the mighty men of David!" he proudly announced, as yet another wave of subjects pressed into the throne room to pledge allegiance to him.

These men, most as old as his father or older, still bore their swords and shields with regality and honor. Forever they had been faithful, and forever faithful they would remain. Although their number had diminished as death had claimed one after another, their corporate love for David had not lessened one whit. And that love asked now that they cast their allegiance to his choice of successor.

"Long live King Solomon!" each gravelly, aging voice willingly intoned, as they each dropped to one knee in a display of fealty before his throne.

Silence hung in the air as they waited for his acknowledgment. His father lightly touched his shoulder as a reminder.

Solomon found his voice and, mustering his most grown-up tone, firmly pronounced, "Rise and go forth in the name of our God." It seemed the right thing to say. His

---

2.   Proverbs 4:23, 25-27.

father smiled. This routine of kingship he would learn. He ventured to relax a bit in order to enjoy the thrill of the moment....

More Instructions

After all the officers of the army had presented themselves, David whispered into Solomon's ear, "I must rest now. Meet me tomorrow morning in the garden." As taxing as today had been, David still had many final instructions to give to his son.

The next day, after morning prayers, as the sun climbed in the eastern sky, father and son met on the rooftop, the fragrant scent of flowers and herbs hanging about them in the air.

"Have you enjoyed the flowers I planted here, Father? Aren't they beautiful?" Solomon asked as he stroked the petals of one after another with his long, slender fingers.

"Yes, yes, they are beautiful," responded David tenderly, "although I must admit I've had little time to enjoy them." He heaved an involuntary sigh. "Maybe when all the kingdom business has been set to rest, I'll have my couch moved up here so that I can appreciate them as they deserve." His face brightened, as another thought struck him. "What a wonderful place to play my lyre and create more music for the Lord!" Then with an apologetic smile, he added, "But perhaps no one will want to hear this old voice anymore by then."

"Nonsense, Father!" remonstrated the boy without hesitation, adjusting the velvet cushion behind David's back. "Your voice will always be loved!"

Just then, Solomon saw a look in his father's eyes that he had witnessed repeatedly throughout his childhood. David was traveling back in spirit to the desert pastures where he had guided his father Jesse's sheep during his own childhood.

"You're not smelling my flowers, are you, Father!" The son exclaimed more than asked. "You're smelling cactus blooms and desert dust!"

At that, they both laughed. There was little David could put over on Solomon, especially in matters of the heart. Each had his own frame of reference for beauty. David's was the wilderness and limitless skies; Solomon's was the formal gardens he loved to create and the beautiful horses in the king's stables. But together, they truly understood beauty.

David cleared his throat. "Now for business...Adonijah's bid for the throne has been subverted and he has pledged allegiance to you. But watch for further treachery and deal with it as you see fit."

He shifted uneasily on his cushioned lounge and continued with a bit of steel in his voice. "Another troublesome person is my commander, Joab. He will need to be dealt with as well. I have never had the courage to discipline him as he deserved. But you are free of the history of his service and intimidation, and you can move swiftly and decisively in disciplining him for his past disobedience in killing Absalom and for disloyalty in backing Adonijah. He is no longer to be feared and likely expects retribution from you."

And on David went, giving Solomon precise instructions regarding the few remaining antagonists he might need to deal with—to remove any encumbrance on his coming rule.

Divine Destiny

The conversation had lasted only an hour, but David was exhausted. However, there was one thing more that must be stressed. He cleared his throat and began.

"My precious son, the most important thing for you to understand is this: Your very life and Israel's future are driven by divine decree, not man's desires. *God* has chosen you for the throne; *God* will keep the land at peace under your rule; *God* will love and discipline you as a beloved son; *God* will guard the throne and power of Israel...but **only** as long as you serve Him with all your heart."

The weight of it all began to settle onto the young monarch's shoulders. "My son," David continued gravely, "if you fail to honor God in all things and allow your heart to be divided in its loyalty, the kingdom will be torn from your family's hands. It is that simple!"

David gripped his son's hands and held them fast, looking him straight in the eyes. "The whole nation is a witness to these conditions, and the whole nation will rise and fall on your choices in response to God's promises." After a long pause for effect, David asked seriously, "Do you understand?"

Solomon gulped and responded more because he had to than because he really understood. "Yes, Father."

"Now help me to my chambers," David whispered with a sigh. "I'm tired."

———————

Traeh twitched nervously from the bowels of the earth.

CHAPTER THREE

ON HIS OWN

W̲hen all of King David's final instructions had been followed, the noble liege died. All Israel grieved—and Solomon most of all.

The night after his father's death, Solomon was inconsolable. Alone in his royal chambers, he wept for hours. However, after midnight, as the crescent moon hung balefully in the sky outside his window, the young king ceased his weeping. He began poring over forty years' worth of parchment that he had discovered tucked away in a cedar chest at the foot of his father's bed. On each piece of parchment were the words to the haunting melodies that David had composed—under the stars, on the run, in peace and in war—over the span of his lifetime. His son, well schooled in the best literature of his day, admired them all tirelessly.

Solomon lifted his head and gazed toward the doorway expectantly. He was not disappointed. His father's voice rang out clear and strong and sweet. "It's as though he is just down the hall, singing to my mother after the evening meal," Solomon whispered. He held his breath, trying to catch every imaginary sound. "How warm his voice, yet somehow cool and distant, as though from some mystical land beyond time!" the boy continued, as the memories hung heavily all around him. "How he loved to sing of his God!" Solomon shook his head in wonderment, and then smiled in spite of himself. And again, "How he loved Jehovah!" He leaned back upon his cushioned divan and listened on. It was as though David were asking God to prepare him for his passage to Heaven.

> *Hide me in the shadow of Your wings.*
> *Hear my cry and grant me courage, O my God!*
> *And I—in righteousness I will see Your face!*
> *O Lord my God, the King of kings.*[3]

And then the music stopped. Abruptly, Solomon found himself alone once more—and once more he fell to weeping.

At the far end of the colonnaded passageway that linked Solomon's chambers to those of his mother's, Bathsheba held her own vigil as she mourned the passing of the man whom she had loved without reservation. In her arms lay David's lyre, silent and solemn. Never again would it resonate with the poignant melodies of the shepherd-king. Never again would anyone's voice accompany its lilting notes and tender tones. The only one who knew how to draw from its seemingly bottomless reservoir of song was no more.

"It will go with him into his grave," she spoke quietly. She gently stroked its worn contours and weathered frame—stained with a shepherd's sweat and desert dust, set with cloudbursts of rain and the hunted warrior's tears.

Buried in Jerusalem

King Solomon spared no expense in providing the most magnificent funeral and burial that could be given. David's tomb on the southern hill within Jerusalem was elaborate, its many rooms filled with rich treasures. Every possible

---

3. Taken from Psalm 17:8b, 15.

deference was given by son to father; honoring his father's name was not a burden.

Just before David's body was sealed away from the world, and darkness became his earthly dwelling, Bathsheba laid his precious lyre beside him.

Together, son and mother embraced their common sorrow. As Solomon sought to comfort her, his own heart stretched to understand the simple love his parents had shared, which had shaped his own destiny. He longed for such a love. And he vowed he would find it.

Final Resolution

Life went on. As Solomon's rule commenced, he did, indeed, have to deal with his stepbrother, Adonijah, who continued to test his authority. The elder brother's foolishness cost him his life. So too was the penalty for all the antagonists about whom David had warned his son. Each time, the troubles they caused were brought upon their own heads. Through everything, Solomon remained fair.

But as he looked out over Jerusalem and watched the multitudes of people milling about—buying and selling, involved in petty squabbles, or laughing at play—he realized that his feelings for them were distant and sterile. Hard as he tried, he couldn't quite sense what was happening within their lives. He knew that he lacked the shepherd's heart that had made his father able to relate so easily to anyone he encountered, especially the common folk.

"He called them his two-legged sheep," the king said to no one in particular. Then shrugging his shoulders, he dismissed the notion of its importance and headed back to court.

This king had never tended sheep, never slept on the ground, never spent endless nights under the stars awaiting a predator's attack or a thief's encroachment. He couldn't understand a tenuous existence at the hand of natural forces.

But he *did* understand power and the propensity of weak men to hunger for it as a substitute for strength of character. And he understood the power of diplomacy with those who already possessed the power to dethrone him or steal his land.

To the south and west of his kingdom lay Egypt, the patient sphinx long awaiting its revenge on Israel for the humiliation caused by the Exodus of Hebrew children under Moses centuries before. Although the might of Egypt had waned during recent periods of civil war, and Israel's had waxed great under David, Solomon still preferred Pharaoh as a friend rather than a foe.

So when a courier brought word to Solomon that Pharaoh was coming with his vast retinue to pay him a visit, the young king called on his advisers for political counsel. When Pharaoh arrived, he would be prepared.

Pharaoh's Arrival

The camel caravan, which had crossed the Sinai Peninsula and the deserts between Egypt and Israel, could be seen for miles, making its measured journey toward Jerusalem. The majestic fortress on the ridge of hills rising above the slender Kidron Valley in the heart of Israel's territories beckoned to Pharaoh as he neared his destination.

Watching from a turret in the western wall of Jerusalem, Solomon was disappointed that the entourage wasn't traveling in Egypt's famed chariots pulled by the most magnificent horses bred in the known world. His father, David, had owned a stable of thoroughbreds, which Adonijah had commandeered for his show of power before

Solomon had been declared king, but Israel's stock was puny in comparison with Pharaoh's. David had taught Solomon that mules were much better suited for travel across Israel's rough terrain, and only camels made sense in the desert. But Solomon preferred being pulled by powerful, sleek horses in the gracious comfort of a chariot to bouncing along on the back of a camel or mule!

On the brilliant spring morning when Pharaoh and his company completed the final leg of their journey, Jerusalem bustled with preparations for the first royal visitors to come during Solomon's young reign. As Pharaoh drew within a mile of the city, the gates were swung open and the king's personal guards sent out on mules to meet him and escort him the rest of the way. Solomon waited pensively in his own royal throne room, dressed in his best robe—tall and handsome—his jeweled crown securely settled upon his head. His thick, wavy, raven hair was neatly trimmed as usual, framing finely chiseled features and fathomless dark eyes. On a throne he had designed just for her and placed next to his after his father's death sat Bathsheba—now gray-haired and retiring, but regal as always.

From the time Pharaoh entered the room until the moment he retired to his lavishly prepared quarters, Solomon's head was in a spin. But somehow, he managed to remain serene and give an appearance of being in command. As his guest exited, he tried to recapture what had just transpired.

His closest adviser, Nathan the prophet, spoke first. "But is it wise, O King, to take a foreign wife, no matter how advantageous the treaty?" It seemed that Nathan often used a question with Solomon to make a statement. That irritated the young king. And so he ignored the warning.

"I will do what will make this land secure, Nathan, and nothing less...wife or no wife," Solomon emphatically answered while refusing to look the prophet in the eye. "This is the way all nations preserve peace these days," he continued firmly, trying to convince himself as well as the old man kneeling before him. "We no longer live in barbarous times!" And then he added more gently as he suddenly caught on to Nathan's concern, "Neither you nor God need worry about my heart being drawn from Him by this wife. I will control my affections!" the naive young king declared.

"Be careful, my liege!" But before Nathan could say more, Solomon arose to leave the room for his own chambers. Passing by the still-kneeling prophet, he patted Nathan encouragingly on the shoulder.

"Don't worry, dear friend, all will be well. You'll see," he turned back to speak softly to Nathan, his father's confidante whom he had loved for as long as he could remember. When he glanced briefly at his mother, he saw as usual the look on her face that said he could do no wrong. That look was all he needed to proceed in forming the liaison.

Signed and Sealed

And so, after much feasting, the treaty was signed and the bride promised in return.

Solomon lay awake for hours that night trying to imagine being married. *A wife already! And Rameses XI's daughter at that! This is amazing!* He had to smile to himself there in the darkness, for he had heard tales of her unsurpassed beauty.

"What harm can there be in it?" he asked aloud. "She will bow to me and show once again the power and glory of the Hebrew God who miraculously delivered us from her forefather's hand." The young king was warming quickly to the whole idea.

And then, mysteriously, a voice not unlike his father's spoke urgently into his heart, and the sands in the hourglass on his nightstand ceased flowing. Time stood still as the voice of Promise Giver spoke. ***Beware, dear boy, the snares of treaties with those who know not My name. Beware the snares of foreign gods that kept your ancestors so long in the wilderness after fleeing the very country with which you consort.*** A pause ensued, and then the final plea, ***Beware, for I love you...*** The voice fell silent.

And the sand flowed again as Solomon shook his head and laughed nervously.

How silly! he thought. *We are no longer fools in the desert! We are no longer confused about our identity, wandering about, homeless and nameless. We need fear nothing... nothing but war*, he grimaced. *And war we will not have, if I can help it!*

In his heart, the transaction was complete. And in his heart, he dreamed that this young girl's love would likewise make him complete.

———————

As Traeh watched with bated breath, the tiny dark shadow in Solomon's heart took on a discernible, however innocent, shape. His lips curled into a grotesque smile as slime oozed from his foul mouth.

Meanwhile, Promise Giver hovered over the boy, loving him as he slept. The battle had only begun.

CHAPTER FOUR

THE GIFT

⤙•⤚

A nd so she came—an intriguing young lady—yet as innocent as the boy. Together they awakened the desires that are the ways of love on earth.

But as much as they shared in affection, Solomon's heart remained empty. When the fascination with his foreign bride subsided, and Queen Adona's exotic ways lost their ability to surprise him, his hunger for love was only stronger.

However, he was bound to her in another way. Having heard of the young king's scholarly bent, Pharaoh had included select volumes of the great wisdom literature of Egypt—the finest perhaps in the world—as part of the dowry that had accompanied the princess. Solomon was captivated by it. He set about devouring the legends and lore—mystical and magical—as fast as his eyes and heart could take them in. Adona happily tutored him in the philosophy of her countrymen and the ways of her religion. This new knowledge quickened the sleeping dreamer in him and created a thirst for something he could not define.

Return to Childhood

Solomon steeped his keen mind and imagination in the intricacies of Egyptian philosophy, religion, and wisdom literature, which was all the rage. At night, however, the tender king would sometimes call his seven Hebrew wise men to meet him in his personal chambers in David's palace after their evening prayers. There in privacy, he'd return to the simplicity of the faith of his childhood as these men would recite again the glories and deeds of the God of his people and of his own young life. It was, perhaps, an unconscious attempt to keep his own spiritual bearings.

He was, after all, the son of the greatest lover of Jehovah his nation had known in some time—a man who knew and understood God's heart.

"And then what happened, Elkaniah?" Solomon would intently query his favorite wise man in the midst of the retelling of a story he knew by heart. At these moments, the child in him was set free. Humoring His Majesty, Elkaniah would pretend to be telling it for the first time ever.

Solomon especially loved hearing over and over the stories of his brave father's conquest of the giant, Goliath, when David was no older than the young king was now. Elkaniah would wax dramatic, setting the stage for young David's fearless facing of the titan from Gath, who had had the gall to challenge Jehovah and His people. Jesse, one of Solomon's palace guards—a rather large man himself—would play the part of the nine-foot tall giant.

"As David crested the last hill," Elkaniah would say slowly, creating great suspense among all who were listening, "and the Valley of Elah lay before him, he was astounded at what he saw. Two mighty armies were facing each other: one boisterous and jaunty, with each man shaking his fist in the air; the other, huddled in a motionless lump. When the battle cry went up, both armies ran to their battle lines—one still defiant, the other intimidated and bewildered." At this, Solomon always shook his head in dismay.

The wonderful storyteller would continue, "So David hurried to get a closer look. Standing at the front of the Philistine army was a gigantic man," at which time Jesse strode with arrogance into the center of the room, flexing his muscles, "whose armor of bronze weighed 125 pounds! A bronze javelin was slung on his back, and the shaft of his spear alone weighed 15 pounds! By the time the young shepherd boy arrived, the Israelites had been quaking in their sandals for forty days, unable to find a comparable champion among their ranks to take on the heavily armed and armor-plated Goliath.

"This made David furious!" the narrative would continue. "The youth, dressed in a simple tunic tied fast at the waist with a leather strap and having only a sling and three small, smooth river stones, ran out to face the giant." On cue, Solomon would jump up and play his father's part, so well had he learned David's lines.

With great bravado, Solomon would shout his lines, "You come against me with sword and spear and javelin, but I come against you in the name of the Lord Almighty, the God of the armies of Israel, whom you have defied. This day the Lord will hand you over to me, and I'll strike you down and cut off your head," at which point the boy would make a slashing motion across his own throat for emphasis, "and the whole world will know that there is a God in Israel! All those gathered here will know that it is not by sword or spear that the Lord saves; for the battle is the Lord's, and He will give all of you into our hands."

Around and around, Solomon would swing an imaginary sling with a single smooth stone in it. At this, Elkaniah would pick up the narrative again. "Swiftly and surely the missile found its mark between the eyes of the giant. How the ground shook at his fall!" Immediately, all seven wise men in the room would shake as though they were about to fall down too! Then Solomon would run over to Jesse—who by then lay on the marble floor of the chamber—and pretend to sever the giant's head from his body.

And so the story went time after time, exactly the same, with the wise men enjoying the play as fully as Solomon. At no other time were they afforded the luxury of pretense and melodrama in the courts of the king. At no other time was life so simple for the boy.

On those nights, after Solomon bid them good night and retired to his bed, he slept soundly, dreaming of angels and dragons warring in the heavenlies—the angels always winning.

His Prayer

With daylight came extraordinary responsibility for the youth—responsibility with which he felt totally unqualified to deal. As much as he desired to obey God, the path to obedience seemed like a maze to the boy. He and Simeon, his blond, curly-headed buddy from childhood, had endless debates about it.

"I hate to say it, but you spend more time studying Egyptian gods than the laws of Moses!" Simeon had blurted out to him in frustration. "How do you expect to know the heart of God in a crisis?" At this remonstrance from his best friend and companion since early childhood, Solomon hung his head. Seeing his opening, Simeon decided to risk voicing another concern. "And when are you going to stop the people from setting up altars to all kinds of gods all over the countryside? You even go there yourself sometimes! Do you think God doesn't see?"

Simeon had struck a nerve on that complaint. Solomon stiffened and glared at Simeon. "I'm David's son, and God's promise is upon me," he declared defensively. "My heart has not left Jehovah! It is just my curiosity that takes me to those altars. They and their gods mean nothing to me," he declared emphatically.

Then the king relaxed and spoke more quietly. "I will back off from going just to please you, though, Simeon," he continued, trying to placate his friend. "I know only Jehovah can help me rule." And then with sincerity he added, "I'd be lost without Him."

Suddenly, a great idea struck him. "Simeon, will you come with me to Gibeon to worship Him and make sacrifices to Him as soon as I can arrange to be away for a few days?" Solomon pleaded with his friend.

And so, the king and the youthful Simeon made the journey to Gibeon—the most important and sanctioned high place—to worship. There the king offered a thousand burnt offerings—in his quest to make things right and guarantee God's blessing.

In God's Presence

That night, as smoke still hung in the air from all the sacrifices, Solomon fell into a deep sleep, exhausted from the day's rituals and prayers. As he relived in dreams the ancient tales of God's goodness toward his people, a Presence—breathtakingly pure and loving—moved into his soul.

Promise Giver's eyes gently roamed through the chambers of the sleeping king's heart. He saw with sorrow the windows of the soul that Solomon had willfully opened, if only a crack, to a world that could entice this heart to sin. He saw the king's hunger for love and mystery, and his inevitable isolation, as a royal monarch, from all the common pressures of life that could teach him quickly to depend upon the strength of God. He saw, too, the seeds of uniqueness sown by his doting parents that could grow into a careless disregard for the statutes of the one true God. And Promise Giver grieved—not for Himself, but for the boy whom He loved.

But He also saw Solomon's loneliness and fear of failure. And so, in His love, He whispered, *Ask for whatever you want Me to give you.*

Solomon, overwhelmed by the serene, yet indescribable Presence who stood before him, replied, "You have shown great kindness to Your servant, my father David, because he was faithful to You and righteous and upright in heart. You have continued this great kindness to him and have given him a son to sit on his throne this very day."

But then the very weight of what he was saying, the weight of the fact that he must rule in his father's stead, overwhelmed him. He felt as though he could never live up to the task. And so he blurted out, "But I am only a little child and do not know how to carry out my duties. Your servant is here among the people You have chosen, a great people, too numerous to count or number!"

Then pleadingly, "So give Your servant a discerning heart to govern Your people and to distinguish between right and wrong. For who is able to govern this great people of Yours?" he concluded.

Promise Giver was pleased that Solomon had asked for this. So He said to him, *Since you have asked for this and not for long life or wealth for yourself, nor have you asked for the death of your enemies but for discernment in administering justice, I will do what you have asked. I will give you a wise and discerning heart, so there will never have been anyone like you, nor will there ever be. Moreover, I will give you what you have not asked for—both riches and honor—so that in your lifetime you will have no equal among kings.*

Promise Giver paused for effect, making sure He had Solomon's complete attention, then continued, *If you walk in My ways and obey My statutes and commands as David your father did, I will give you a long life.*

In the next instant, Solomon awoke—and he realized it had been a dream. But he would never be the same. A depth of insight had invaded his soul.

In joy and great gratitude, he returned to Jerusalem, stood before the Ark of the Lord's Covenant, and sacrificed burnt offerings and fellowship offerings. Then he gave a feast for all his court.

Sorrow Again

A week later, Bathsheba joined David in death. Solomon grieved from the depths of his heart the loss of the only one on earth whom he felt understood and unconditionally loved him.

But in his sorrow, the young king felt a new Presence— that of the One who had answered his cry at Gibeon. He was not alone when the tomb was sealed once more, ending his childhood forever.

On the starless night that followed, Solomon again heard the phantom singing from his parents' now-empty quarters. His father's voice rang out again, this time in subdued tones, a lingering sadness surrounding each note:

> *The Lord is my Shepherd, I shall not be in want.*
> *He makes me lie down in green pastures,*
> *He leads me beside quiet waters,*
> *He restores my soul.*
> *He guides me in paths of righteousness*
> *for His name's sake.*
> *Even though I walk*

through the valley of the shadow of death,
I will fear no evil,
for You are with me;
Your rod and Your staff,
they comfort me...

And the sorrowing king was truly comforted as the Presence of his father's Shepherd embraced him as well.

―――――――――――

Traeh shuddered and withdrew into his self-imposed and eternal hell. The mists of death embraced him and he choked on the thought of Promise Giver's allegiance to this vulnerable young man, David's son. His only consolation was the camaraderie of his wizened demons, who ceaselessly brought to him new ways to deceive and degrade the mortal liege upon the throne of Israel.

CHAPTER FIVE

PROMISES KEPT

I t wasn't long before Promise Giver's gift of wisdom was put to the test. Two quarreling prostitutes were brought to the king to petition him for justice. One of them was allowed to speak first. She began matter-of-factly, "My lord, this woman and I live in the same house. I had a baby while she was there with me. The third day after my child was born, this woman also had a baby. We were alone; there was no one in the house but the two of us.

"During the night," she continued, with tears welling up in her eyes, "this woman's son died because she lay on him. So she got up in the middle of the night and took my son from my side while I was asleep. She put him by her breast and put her dead son by my breast. The next morning, I got up to nurse my son—and he was dead! But when I looked at him closely in the morning light, I saw that it wasn't the son I had borne." At this she broke down sobbing.

The other woman abruptly burst out, "No! The dead one is yours; the living one is mine!" And so they argued before the king.

Solomon looked at them both intently and replied, "Bring me a sword." So the puzzled guard to whom he had given the order brought his own sword and stood before the king. Solomon then solemnly commanded: "Cut the living child in two and give half to one and half to the other."

Everyone in the courtroom gasped. Filled with compassion for the child, the woman whose son was alive called out to the king, "Please, my lord, give her the living baby! Don't kill him!"

But the other snapped coldly, "Neither I nor you shall have him. Cut him in two!"

All in attendance waited with bated breath for the king's ruling. "Give the living baby to the first woman," he ordered quietly. "Do not kill him; *she* is his mother."

The story spread like wildfire throughout Israel, and when the people heard the verdict the king had given, they held the king in awe because they saw that he had wisdom from God to administer justice.

Promise Giver smiled from the distant heavens, while His eyes continued to search the king's heart.

The Time Had Arrived

Meanwhile, all the king set his hand to do prospered, and Israel became stronger than ever, and very wealthy. The treaties that his father had made with all the countries along her border stood firm, and each was happy to pay tribute to Solomon in exchange for his protection.

And then, one sunny morning, Solomon arose with a "knowing" in his heart. It was time to commence the building of the temple for Jehovah, the God of his fathers, who would enable him to rule with wisdom. The land was at peace, the people were content, and all the world seemed at his feet. Now history was to be written for which he would be further remembered. But he would need help.

Now Hiram, King of Tyre, had always been on friendly terms with David. And Hiram also had many craftsmen and natural resources that Solomon needed. Fortunately, when Hiram heard that Solomon had been anointed king to succeed his father David, he decided to send his envoy to Israel to further cement peace. The timing was perfect. After great ceremony was made between the two kings' representatives during the visit, Solomon composed the following message and sent it back with the envoy to Hiram:

You know that because of the wars waged against my father David from all sides, he could not build a temple for the name of the Lord his God until the Lord put his enemies under his feet. But now the Lord my God has given me rest on every side, and there is no adversary or disaster. I intend, therefore, to build a temple for the name of the Lord my God, as the Lord told my father David, when He said, "Your son whom I will put on the throne in your place will build the temple for My name."

So give orders that cedars of Lebanon be cut for me. My men will work with yours, and I will pay you for your men whatever wages you set. You know that we have no one so skilled in felling timber as the Sidonians.

When Hiram heard Solomon's message, he was greatly pleased and said, "Praise be to the Lord today, for He has given David a wise son to rule over this great nation."

And then he sent this reply to Solomon:

I have received the message you sent me and will do all you want in providing the cedar and pine logs. My men will haul them down from Lebanon to the sea, and I will float them in rafts by sea to the place you specify. There I will separate them and you can take them away. And you are to grant my wish by providing food for my royal household.

So began their business relationship. Hiram kept Solomon supplied with all the cedar and pine logs he wanted, and Solomon gave Hiram about 375 bushels of wheat as food for his household, in addition to 115,000 gallons of pressed olive oil. Solomon continued to do this for Hiram year after year.

The Temple

As Solomon studied in earnest the temple plans, he remembered an odd instruction his father had given him. "Son," David had said, "the site of the temple is holy and must not be violated by the sounds of construction. On Mt. Moriah where it is to be built—where Abraham offered Isaac and where I made a sacrifice to stop the plague on my people brought about by my pride in counting my fighting men—there must not be the pounding of hammers or the grinding of chisels."

"But how can we build it without tools?" had been Solomon's incredulous reply. "You're asking me to do the impossible!"

David had chuckled and then grown serious. "It's really quite simple: Plan very carefully the dimensions of every stone and timber." Putting his arm around the boy's shoulders and cocking his head to look him in the eyes, David had continued, "Then instruct your workers to shape the stones at the quarry, and cut the timber at its point of delivery by King Hiram. When all is brought to Mt. Moriah, you will put the temple together as you would a huge puzzle." Then the old king had laughed, "I daresay you have the mind for it, my boy. If anyone can do it, you can." Seeing the look of doubt on Solomon's face he added reassuringly, "And you'll have all the best masons and carpenters in the land to help you."

Solomon's shoulders had relaxed at this last statement, and he had suddenly felt up to the task—even anxious to begin! But his father had cautioned him to wait for the right time after the establishment of his own reign.

And the time had arrived. After the finest craftsmen had been enlisted, the highest quality quarries chosen, laborers selected, and plans explained, the work began at sites away from the temple mount. The king estimated that he had more than enough gold in the royal treasury to overlay everything—from the ornately carved walls and pillars, to the altar and all the furnishings and utensils that would be used by the priests in worship. Even the sockets for the doors would be gold-plated.

All would be assembled when ready.

Busy Times

Solomon's days were a flurry of activity from sunup to sundown. He held court and conferred with dignitaries or his own advisors as needed, while still overseeing every aspect of the design and construction of the temple. Whenever he could, he traveled to the work sites as well. Somehow he still managed to study the rising volume of wisdom literature that was coming from Egypt, Phoenicia, and China. He even began writing his own in a form he called *the proverb*.

He also found himself quite adept at composing complex riddles. A friendship was growing between Hiram and Solomon, and the two of them were soon making a game of it—challenging each other with riddles, betting everything from gold to horses on who could unravel the other's riddle. So were the games that wealthy people played in those days.

Meanwhile, the temple began to rise from its carefully laid foundation of perfectly fitted white stones, set deep into the soil to guarantee an enduring support for the ponderous edifice. Towering above all else in Jerusalem, and with over twice the horizontal dimensions of the Tent of Meeting that had been pitched in the middle of Jerusalem by David, the Dwelling was an imposing sight, as magnificent as Solomon had desired. The gold with which it was completely covered shone in the sunlight, dazzling the eyes of anyone who looked upon it.

Its two inner chambers—the Holy Place and the Most Holy Place—were surrounded with yet another exterior wall that rose three stories into the air. Around this exterior and on each of the three levels, were thirty rooms with passages connecting them. They would be for storage and for use by the priests. A massive common roof arched over the entire complex construction.

Its interior walls were lined with the finest cedar boards, and the floors were covered with pine—then all was overlaid with gold. Beautiful engravings of pomegranates, palm trees, and gourds—covered with gold—adorned every wall, door, and pillar throughout the temple. Hanging over every doorway in the vast building were delicate, flowing veils of blue, purple, and scarlet of the brightest and softest linen, with the most curious flowers etched upon them.

The inner sanctuary within the temple, the Most Holy Place where the Ark of the Covenant of the Lord would be placed, was overlaid with pure gold, and the altar, with cedar. A pair of cherubim made of olive wood—stunning angels, each fifteen feet high with outspread wings that were seven-and-a-half feet long—were put inside this sanctuary. The wing of one cherub touched one wall, and the wing of the other touched the opposing wall, while their other wings met tip to tip in the middle of the room. They were, of course, overlaid with gold.

From foundation to eaves, every stone had been cut to size and trimmed with a saw on its inner and outer faces at the quarry. Not a single sound of hammer, chisel, or saw was heard upon the sacred mount.

Begun in the fourth year of King Solomon's reign, the temple of the Lord was finished in the eleventh year—all according to the specifications David had given Solomon on that day they had walked together on Mt. Moriah.

The Day of Joy

Excitement was at a fever pitch the day the temple was completed. The king sent word out to all the elders of Israel, all the heads of the tribes, and all the chiefs of the Israelite families to accompany the Ark of the Covenant from Jerusalem to Mt. Moriah. The very focal point of their worship—that over which the Presence of God had hovered when Israel had escaped from Egypt over five hundred years before—would finally be given a permanent dwelling. This symbol of God's power and authority that had moved with the children of Israel in the wilderness for the forty years following the Exodus, the Ark that had brought blessing to God's people time and time again, would have a home at last.

While the priests and Levites carried the Ark on their shoulders by the long poles that had been inserted in brass rings at the corners of the Ark, the king and all the people went ahead to the mount to sacrifice so many sheep and cattle that they could not be counted or recorded!

When the Ark reached the temple, it was taken to the Most Holy Place and put beneath the wings of the cherubim. What happened next brought all the people—even the children—to their knees. As the priests withdrew from the sanctuary, the cloud that had led the Ark by day in the wilderness filled the temple of the Lord and flowed out of its portals! The priests could not perform their duties because the glory of the Lord was overwhelming. In the presence of such majesty and mystery, all they could do was fall on their faces in worship.

Nighttime Reflections

That night, as Solomon lay on his bed, jubilant but exhausted, the events of the day played over and over in his head. His own prayer to God before his people, had come from somewhere deep in his belly—deep in the heart of all he was and all he believed. In front of the whole assembly of Israel, he had spread out his hands toward Heaven and prayed:

"O Lord, God of Israel," he had begun, "there is no God like You in Heaven above or on earth below...You who keep Your covenant of love with Your servants who continue wholeheartedly in Your way." How his heart had pounded with love in return for all God had given him the strength to do in building the great temple, the fulfillment of his beloved father's fondest dream!

And what else had he prayed as he had been held captive by the power and majesty of the Lord's holy Presence? He remembered snatches of it... "Hear the supplication of Your servant and of Your people Israel when they pray toward this place. Hear from Heaven, Your dwelling place, and when You hear, forgive."

How strange. He couldn't remember ever having prayed about forgiveness before.

As he drifted off to sleep, his great prayer of intercession—which he could remember only in pieces—rolled over his soul like the waves of the sea. In his dreams, the prayer for forgiveness was inextricably wrapped around images of despair—images that, strain as he might to see them, he could not distinguish. All was shrouded in mystery.

The Challenge

When he awoke in the morning, all he could remember was the blessing he had spoken over the whole assembly of Israel, which he had rehearsed for many days before the event: "Praise be to the Lord who has given rest to His people Israel just as He promised...may He turn our hearts to Him, to walk in all His ways...and may these words of mine, which I have prayed before the Lord, be near to the Lord our God day and night...so that all the peoples of the earth may know that the Lord is God and that there is no other."

And then, just as Jehovah had challenged him again that day as at Gibeon, he sternly turned the challenge toward the sea of people gathered around the massive golden pillars and overflowing down the temple steps: "But your hearts must be fully committed to the Lord our God, to live by His decrees and obey His commands as at this time."

If the people will just obey, he whispered to himself, unconsciously furrowing his brow for an instant.

The Dedication

The next day, dreams forgotten, the king and all Israel with him celebrated the dedication of the temple. He consecrated the middle part of the courtyard in front of the temple of the Lord and there offered burnt offerings, grain offerings, and the fat of the fellowship offerings. And on went the celebration—a vast assembly of people from Lebo Hamath to the Wadi of Egypt—for fourteen days. On the fifteenth day, he sent them away. They blessed the king and went home, joyful and glad in heart for all the good things the Lord had done for His servant David and His people Israel.

Subtle Provision

That night, with the Presence of Jehovah heavy in the air, Solomon's conscience was pierced. Uneasily, he thought about his Egyptian wife, Queen Adona, living in the palace that David had built, now Solomon's home as well.

"She's not from our nation," he proclaimed as though the thought had just occurred to him. "And I've placed her in the palace of the king who served only Jehovah! She shouldn't be there!" Immediately, his mind sought a solution.

"I must build a separate palace for her, a place that is not a sacred site," he declared emphatically. "Then all will be well."

And so, with little time taken to rest, Solomon set about designing her home. His artistic talent and architectural genius would be truly challenged by the task. He had come to realize that this edifice must not only house the queen's luxurious suite, but also courtrooms, banquet halls, a great many bedchambers, and, of course kitchens and servants' quarters. There was no time or space to attempt two or three different structures; they could all be contained in this one elaborate building. Without doubt, more than the eleven years it took to erect the temple would be required. The enormity of the task was a bit daunting.

Slumped over his initial sketches, he rubbed his temples to beat back the pressure of the project. But there was a greater difficulty: The fact was that his heart simply wasn't captivated by this project as it had been by the design and construction of Jehovah's Dwelling. For one thing, his father hadn't left plans or materials for such a building. He would have to call again upon King Hiram for help and somehow rally the energy of his workers once again.

But more than that, he lacked the passion for it that had carried him throughout the building of the temple for Jehovah. The anointing of God was missing.

Just thinking about it made him tired.

However, a slow smile spread over the ever-lurking Traeh's wizened countenance at the mention of a palace for Adona. "He will have a place now for his mistakes. How convenient..." he croaked.

CHAPTER SIX

IN PURSUIT OF LOVE

O ne full year had passed since the dedication of the temple, and Solomon suddenly missed his old friend. He summoned Simeon. They had rarely seen each other during that year, and much had changed—especially for Simeon. He had grown up and become a husband. His parents— knowing him well and understanding the kind of woman with whom he would be happiest—selected Anna. She was steady and true and full of an inner joy that would brighten the hardest of days. All their friends declared it "…a match made in Heaven." And Simeon loved her dearly.

Though a great deal had changed for Simeon, he and the king were friends who could pick right up where they had left off at their last meeting.

"So you're happy, are you, my friend?" Solomon asked as he passed Simeon a bowl of firm, succulent grapes and a plate of silken cheese. The two young men lounged lazily on the divans in the reception hall of David's palace, for a moment, undisturbed.

Simeon, dressed more handsomely than Solomon had ever seen him before—his tunic crisp and well-fitting, his sandals of soft, new leather—looked up shyly and broke into a broad smile. "Happier than I ever dreamed I could be! Anna is wonderful! And we may soon be parents as well," he added proudly.

Solomon eyed his contented friend and heaved a sigh. "Why can't I find a good Jewish girl like that?" Then thinking of Adona, he added wistfully, "A foreign woman cannot truly warm my heart or bring me joy, no matter how hard she may try."

Simeon started to answer, but the king interrupted as he suddenly leaned earnestly toward him and spoke again. "I am suffocating here under all this pressure. If I venture into the streets, I'm mobbed by people asking me to solve their disputes. Isn't it enough that I hold court every day?" Not waiting for an answer, he continued dismally. "Sometimes I wonder about the value of all this wisdom! While others find peace, my heart has lost its moorings. I need to get away where no one knows me. But how?" he finished in despair.

His friend listened sympathetically and thoughtfully. Then his soft brown eyes brightened as a great idea came into his head.

"Travel in disguise!" he said softly, trying to control his glee at the prospect. "Dress like a commoner and go out into the country for some peace and quiet. Take just enough provisions so you'll not need to beg, but not so many that you tempt robbers to attack you." Then he remembered, "Didn't your father, King David, do that once when he wanted to sneak back to Bethlehem and relive being a shepherd?" Obviously pleased with himself, Simeon stopped and waited for the king's reaction to his clever scheme.

Solomon nearly stopped breathing as he listened to Simeon's outrageous idea. "Yes, he did!" he quickly responded, smiling broadly as he recalled his father's humorous and touching telling of the tale. "But dare I?" he asked himself. After a pregnant pause, he finally chimed in, "Why not?" And then, "I'll do it!" he announced. After slapping his friend unceremoniously on the back, he quickly got to his feet, intent upon setting the bold plan into action as soon as possible.

The King's Plans

But Solomon's life was more complicated than David's had been. Every moment of his day was committed to some activity, and he would be missed immediately and by many. He'd have to take a tack other than simple disappearance.

After explaining to Adona that he'd be away for a few days checking his holdings, he called a meeting of his inner circle of counselors. After cursory greetings were exchanged and refreshments served, he cleared his throat and began to set the stage for his escape.

"As you all know, I own many vineyards around the nation that I have never even seen," he stated matter-of-factly. "It's time that I paid my tenants a visit, don't you think?"

Barak, a gray-headed and ever-practical counselor of the court countered brusquely, "Let your overseers check on them and give you a report, Your Majesty."

"Ah, but that's not the same as a personal visit from me, now is it?" The king smiled a bit condescendingly. "After all they do for me, they at least deserve an expression of gratitude straight from my lips."

Before anyone else could chime in, he concluded: "There are no foreign dignitaries scheduled to visit until fall, nor any cases I must review that can't be postponed a few days." He stood to his full height and spoke more warmly, "It will be a restful trip for me and a very welcome change of pace."

"You deserve a respite, O King," Elijah, an old friend of his father's responded solemnly. "You have spent yourself in service to your people during these past twelve years— far beyond what any other monarch of your youthfulness could have managed. And you have ruled your people with wisdom." Looking encouragingly at each in the circle of advisors, he urged the others to agree. "We all wish that you follow your judgment in this issue." Turning his eyes again to Solomon, he concluded gently, "Take the trip, Son."

They all then nodded dutifully in agreement.

"It's settled then!" Solomon said with pleasure. "I'll leave in the morning. I'll choose my own companions and guards. All will be simply arranged, and I'll return in seven days." He stopped and looked at them with deliberateness and added, "I prefer, however, that word of my trip not be noised abroad. Is that understood?" Each man nodded assent.

At that, he dismissed them. They bowed and wished him a fine trip, then filed out of the chamber.

Preparations

The next day, Solomon set about making his daring escapade a reality. He cleverly gave the impression that he had chosen guards and traveling companions, while making no such arrangements. He would leave alone under the cover of darkness.

He summoned one of the palace servants to secure a worn linen tunic and leather belt, sandals, white cloth for a head covering and a woven band with which to secure it, and a shepherd's staff. When the youth cast him a quizzical look, he fabricated a story.

"It's for a play for the royal family," he responded. "We get precious little entertainment!" he added, chuckling a bit and patting the lad on the shoulder confidentially. The boy, awed by a touch from the legendary king, promptly forgot any questions he had had.

When the youth returned, he had a goatskin canteen for water and a sling, both to be tied onto the leather belt, as well as a sheepskin coat.

"Even in a play, every shepherd needs these things," beamed the boy, obviously pleased with himself for anticipating the requirements of an authentic shepherd's costume. He lingered a bit, hoping for more conversation with the king, but Solomon laughed, rumpled his hair and dismissed him. He bowed and began his exit, but with a disappointed look on his round face. That look made the king laugh again.

"Off with you, my boy! And thank you!" he added.

After the door closed behind the youth, Solomon removed his outer garments and curiously eyed the apparel that had been brought to him.

"So this is what my father wore all those years on the run from King Saul!" As he picked up the sheepskin coat to examine it, the odor of sheep assaulted his senses. "Whew!" he exclaimed, wrinkling his nose. "I wonder how long it will take for me to get used to this disgusting smell!" But in spite of the odor, he was very glad the lad had thought to bring it. He'd have frozen in the desert without it, even during this warm season. The desert had a way of betraying a hot traveler after the sun went down. With the extremes, one must reckon. He'd not thought of that but had been rescued by the boy's common sense.

"How can I be so wise and still so stupid?" he asked his reflection in the mirror. *It's probably not the last time I'll ask myself that question*, he absently mused.

After donning all the clothing and adjusting the head covering made secure with the braided fabric, he looked at himself again in the mirror and was amazed at the transformation. He actually looked like a shepherd...and smelled a bit like one as well!

"Well, almost," he commented ruefully as he looked down at his soft, white hands with their carefully groomed nails. His pale face was also a problem. "A few days roughing it outdoors in the desert will complete the ruse," he concluded with satisfaction.

Leaving

When the household was asleep and the guards were caught up in their nightly ritual of swapping stories among themselves, Solomon made his escape. In his disguise, and with a pouch of provisions slung over his shoulder and a lantern in one hand, he slipped out of the palace through a secret passageway that King David had built into the palace wall to provide an escape in case of siege. It eventually connected with the aqueduct system that the former king and his men had used a generation before to invade and wrest the city from its previous inhabitants, the Jebusites. Along this damp, slippery, slimy route, he made his way slowly so as not to lose his footing.

As the stars began to appear in the velvety night sky, the king emerged, relieved to breathe fresh air once again. After extinguishing his lantern and hiding it behind a rock at the mouth of the tunnel, he circled around to the eastern gate where a stable hand was supposed to have a sturdy donkey waiting for an anonymous patron who would pay him well for his trouble. He was not disappointed. A lad leaned against the outer wall, idly kicking stones with his left foot, the reins to a handsome donkey held loosely in his right hand. The boy had no idea with whom he would be doing business that night.

The stable boy was fooled by the king's clever disguise and happily exchanged the strong young donkey for the coins offered him. Solomon then slung a rolled sleeping mat and saddlebags of simple provisions onto the back of the beast and headed out into the night.

No questions had been asked. He was free!

———————

Curiously Traeh watched the young king's every move. "What is the foolish dreamer up to now?" he hissed, his eyes darting nervously to and fro over the desert landscape.

CHAPTER SEVEN

THE ADVENTURE

The king made his bed under the stars that night. His destination was the hill country of Ephraim, about forty miles north of Jerusalem, where he owned many vineyards. It was an arbitrary destination, but one far enough away that he'd never be recognized.

Unaccustomed to sleeping on the ground, he tossed and turned for hours, trying to get comfortable. Every stone, however small, seemed determined to disrupt his rest.

"How can shepherds *do* this night after night?" he muttered in frustration. But finally, he slept, although fitfully, being startled by every sound in the wind.

As the sun rose, driving back the darkness and invading his restless reprieve, he awoke—sore and stiff. Awkwardly, he managed to get to his feet, realizing that he was chilled to the bone despite the smelly sheepskin he had put on. "Tonight, a fire," he decided then and there. It certainly made sense, but then he groaned when he remembered that he didn't know how to make a fire in the wilderness!

As he alternately walked and rode his donkey over rocks and around scrubby, prickly desert brush, the sun beat relentlessly down upon him. Becoming tanned was no problem; preventing sunburn was, however. Carefully, he arched the front of his head covering and tugged it lower over his brow, forming a sunshield. Still, his face burned as it tanned, the sun being reflected off the sand and up into his face.

By noon of the second day, he was regretting the trip. Sore, sunburned, filthy and nearly out of water and provisions, he began to wonder if his little adventure would cost him his life! About then, he spotted a cluster of sheep on the horizon.

"Ah, where there are sheep, there will be a shepherd. Jehovah has not forgotten me!"

Getting His Bearings

Benjamin, the sturdy shepherd whose age Solomon couldn't venture a guess, drew water for him from an ancient well near the equally ancient acacia tree nearby. The strange little man informed the dusty king that he had drifted west of his planned route, but was very near the village of Kephirah, where he could take lodging and restock his provisions. Then, if he headed northeast to get back on course, Gibeon would be directly ahead of him.

How strange it will be to revisit Gibeon in this condition! He smiled to himself, remembering his anointing there as king nearly thirteen years ago. *How different my world is now*, he sighed inwardly, *and how innocent I was then!*

The Village

The weary king made Kephirah by sundown. Since the villagers weren't used to visitors, the dusty traveler was a curiosity to them. His first stop was the well in the center of the village. While children stopped playing to stare and young women held their veils over their faces and skirted him to return to their mothers, there was one person who spoke to him—Moshe, the village carpenter. As they both cupped their hands in the cold water and drew it up to splash it onto their hot faces, the carpenter asked a simple question: "Are you hungry?"

Solomon suddenly felt hunger deep in his belly, and he answered instinctively, "I certainly am!"

"Then, come home with me," Moshe said with a smile. "We don't have much, but what we have, Miriam makes fit for a king!" he then laughed, little knowing that it was for a king she would indeed be preparing dinner.

What he witnessed that night in the carpenter's home amazed him. Peace and respect reigned. With no luxuries, no grand food or fancy clothing, this family of seven—children ranging in age from two to fourteen years old—lived lovingly within a two-room sod and reed house. And it wasn't long before Solomon realized that Miriam was several months pregnant with their sixth child.

The faithfulness he saw in Moshe and Miriam's eyes whenever they looked at each other was what struck him the most. The willing obedience of the children was equally impressive. Moshe spoke in gentle, yet firm, tones that each child immediately heeded—but without fear. Miriam served them all with gracious generosity and a sweetness he had rarely witnessed in royal circles.

As they visited around the table that night, Solomon averted attention away from himself by asking his host an endless string of questions. As long as he could keep Moshe talking, he was safe from discovery. Fortunately, the middle-aged carpenter was happy to oblige him. Rarely did anyone else query him about his life. Everything was known already in this little village where he had lived since he was born.

"Carpentry is a fine occupation, but what I enjoy most is recording the events of our village," Moshe shyly admitted after his trust had grown strong enough in this visitor for him to be really open.

"Really?" the king's interest was piqued, startled that this common man could read and write.

"History is important, even in a little village like ours," Moshe asserted with conviction. "Someday my great-great-grandchildren will read about how we are living right here today because of what I am recording." He looked proudly around the table at his children.

Suddenly, Moshe blushed. "I'm talking too much and making you weary," he apologized, rising from the table. "It's time for bed. You must be exhausted," he concluded, turning his attention at last to his guest.

"You have certainly not wearied me in the least!" Solomon assured him. "Indeed, such subjects refresh me. I, too, enjoy recording the events and thoughts of our day."

This last remark surprised Moshe and he turned back to the table.

Solomon continued, "In fact, if you have a piece of parchment I may have, and a writing tool I may use, I'd like to record what I want to remember about you and your family, if you don't mind."

Moshe broke out in a big grin. "We're honored. I'll get them for you right away."

Alone with His Thoughts

By candlelight, the tired, dusty king began mulling over what he had learned that day. As he sat in the quieted, peaceful, simple house, the sounds of "shalom" having faded into rest, Solomon thought of the respect he had seen others give Moshe that day—from the well to his home. Using literary styles that were becoming popular in Hebrew poetry, he wrote:

> *A good name is more desirable than great riches;*
> *to be esteemed is better than silver or gold.*[4]

---

4.   Proverbs 22:1.

Then the round, pretty face of Miriam invaded the room, and he wrote further:

A wife of noble character is her husband's crown,
but a disgraceful wife is like decay in his bones.[5]

The eldest son, Ben, provoked another proverb:

A wise son brings joy to his father,
but a foolish son grief to his mother.[6]

What a sight he would have been to his counselors back in Jerusalem! There he sat, writing by candlelight in a sod house in an obscure village in the hills...a sun-burned and dirty stranger with a quill in his hand, writing of wisdom!

And he began to wonder. *Where does wisdom play into this adventure? What is truly the hunger that gnaws at my heart? Why is contentment so elusive for me, who has everything, and such a staple for Moshe who has so little?*

Over the years, Solomon's head had actually ached at times from all his studying and questing for more.

Then, as though being whispered by the shadow he cast against the gray-brown wall behind him, the voice of Promise Giver spoke. It somehow sounded like his father's, and yet also like the same voice that had spoken to him out of his dream at Gibeon and changed his life forever with the Gift. This voice came to him when he most needed counsel.

What had his father, David, told him? "God will be a father to you. He will love you and discipline you as a son."

---

5.   Proverbs 12:4.
6.   Proverbs 10:1.

The love, he felt. The discipline? Perhaps his wisdom would keep him from needing that.

Solomon's mind wandered to Hiram with whom he exchanged proverbs and riddles for entertainment. He thought also of the adoration of the people for his wisdom—adoration that bordered on worship.

"Has my wisdom become a commodity?" he whispered aloud. "Do they see only what I can produce out of it for their amusement or national pride? Does anyone actually love me?"

A chill rushed down his spine and Traeh lunged at his golden opportunity. Into the king's lonely heart—into the hairline fissure that had already snaked its way through its center—he hissed, *Never will anyone be good enough to adequately love a man like you. You are far above all other mortals. Your hungers will never be satisfied by what fills the bellies of these simple people...*

Traeh ceased his shrouded taunt and left the king slumped over the rough wooden table in the center of the suddenly stark room.

The loneliness that stole into Solomon's heart consumed him, and huge tears fell from his eyes onto his writing. He rolled up all the parchments but one and tucked them under his belt, rose sadly to his feet, and stepped out into the night with the sack of fresh provisions—which Miriam had given him before retiring—slung over his shoulder. After gathering his donkey and his gear from the shed behind the house, he trudged off toward his next destination—Gibeon. There was no rest for the desolate king that night.

Promise Giver was waiting for him at Gibeon. As the miserable king fell exhausted to the ground under a massive acacia tree at the gates of the village, the Presence washed over his soul, driving back despair and flooding his body with precious sleep.

When he awoke, the Presence was still there—and he knew it. For the first time he realized for himself that the wisdom he possessed was *not* a commodity, but the Spirit of One yet to come—perhaps even the Promise of which his dear father had sung so often and so long ago. Though he sensed this, he still didn't *understand* it.

Back in Kephirah

When Moshe rose early that morning anxious for more conversation with this mysterious stranger, he was dismayed to find him gone without a trace...except for a gold coin and a scrap of parchment that had been left upon the table.

First, he read the words on the parchment. They were:

> *He who finds a wife finds what is good*
> *and receives favor from the Lord.*[7]

Moshe's face lit up with a broad smile.

Then, remembering the coin, he reached out and picked it up. His jaw dropped as he stared at it. Never before had he seen one of such value.

---

7.   Proverbs 18:22.

CHAPTER EIGHT

JOSHUA

Solomon slept under the stars that night, a deep and dreamless sleep, cradled in the arms of Promise Giver and the One to Come. In the morning, he was in no hurry to get up. Indeed, the Presence upon him drew him irresistibly to reflect upon his life and to look within his own heart—something he had been avoiding for some time. He had feared that the sense of loss hidden there would be more than he could bear.

He missed his precious mother and father. He missed the long talks with them—about life and how to live it. Now that he desperately needed counsel from others, it was not there for him. Instead, others always expected counsel *from* him as though he existed to make their lives more comprehensible—while his grew increasingly *in*comprehensible.

Regardless...he missed them—especially his father.

As he propped himself up against the rough bark of the tree near where he had been sleeping, the Presence wrapped the lonely king in comfort, and his father's words—written when he, too, had been lonely—echoed in his heart:

> *O Lord, You have searched me and You know me.*
> *You know when I sit and when I rise;*
> *You perceive my thoughts from afar.*

You discern my going out and my lying down;
You are familiar with all my ways.
Before a word is on my tongue
You know it completely, O Lord.
You hem me in—behind and before;
You have laid Your hand upon me.
Such knowledge is too wonderful for me,
too lofty for me to attain.
Where can I go from Your Spirit?
Where can I flee from Your presence?
If I go up to the heavens, You are there;
If I make my bed in the depths, You are there.
If I rise on the wings of the dawn,
If I settle on the far side of the sea,
Even there Your hand will guide me,
Your right hand will hold me fast.[8]

And Solomon's heart was strangely warmed.

A Curious Companion

The provisions he had obtained from Moshe and Miriam would last only two days—long enough to reach the little town of Shunam in the hill country of Ephraim, so he decided to press on.

By following a course a little east of due north and through the lowlands, the traveling was easier and water for him and his donkey was more plentiful. About twenty miles beyond Gibeon—out of his sheer hunger for human companionship—the now-browned and properly desert-initiated king joined up with an old man and his donkey traveling the same route. His name was Joshua, and he looked ancient enough to have actually been his namesake—the

---

8. Psalm 139:1-10.

great warrior who had led the children of Israel into the Promised Land centuries before.

Solomon liked Joshua immediately, although he had never before met anyone who even closely resembled the tart old man. The fellow knew his own mind and wasn't afraid to say what was on it without a second thought. He had strong opinions on every subject under the sun.

"So what do you think of the young King Solomon?" the king casually inquired.

Joshua intently studied the rocks along the way for several minutes without answering. Solomon wondered if he *would* answer. After a hacking cough shook his bent frame and a moment more passed as he regained his composure, he switched the reins of the donkey he was leading from one hand to the other, and then answered.

"Not much," he said unceremoniously.

Keeping his anger in check and yielding instead to his curiosity, Solomon rejoined, " 'Not much?' Why do you say such a thing!"

Joshua, surprised at his young, well-spoken companion's shock at his reply, added, "Now, don't get me wrong! Being a king is no easy matter, and he seems to be making some pretty good decisions—especially in building the Dwelling for Jehovah." Then with a chuckle, he added, "And I hear he's planning to build a new home for Pharaoh's daughter. I'd say getting her out of David's palace is smart, too."

Then the old man cocked his bearded head to the side, eyeing a hawk that had just taken off from a brush-covered ledge to his right beyond Solomon. After pursing his lips and wrinkling his nose, he continued carefully, "He seems uncertain, you know?"

" 'Uncertain?' " Solomon queried, his brow furrowed and a confused look on his face.

Joshua stopped and looked at him as though he would begin laughing the next moment. "Must you repeat everything I say?"

Solomon regrouped and answered steadily, "I'm sorry. You just surprised me."

"Well, that's just the matter at hand. I think our highly esteemed and 'wise' king will one day surprise us—*and himself*."

Before Solomon could respond, Joshua abruptly changed the subject. "It hasn't rained in a month, you know."

Apparently, he was through talking about the king.

That Night

After Joshua had fallen asleep and was snoring contentedly on his bedroll on the other side of the fire they had built, Solomon pulled his parchment from his saddlebag. He thoughtfully wrote:

> *An honest answer is like a kiss on the lips.*
> *Like an earring of gold or an ornament of fine gold*
> *is a wise man's rebuke to a listening ear.*[9]

He knew he would be wondering for a long time what Joshua meant by "uncertain."

Parting Ways

As much as Solomon desired to continue their conversation of yesterday, by mid-morning of the new day, Joshua's

---

9.   Proverbs 24:26; 25:12.

destination was to take him due west, while Solomon had to continue north. They bid farewell, both saying they hoped to meet again.

The hills rose up ahead of him—gently rolling, their sides covered with long, neat rows of grape vines stretching away as far as the eye could see. What lush beauty after the barrenness of the desert behind him!

So this is the land given by Jehovah to the sons of Ephraim after the Wilderness Journey. They did well! he thought to himself as he surveyed the fertile landscape.

"These vines are tall enough to find shade beneath!" the weary king stated aloud as he tethered Marcus, his affectionately named donkey. He then sank to the ground by the nearest row.

The vines were carefully tied to posts made of acacia wood to keep them from trailing on the ground and spoiling. The branches—trimmed back in early spring to increase their strength and fruitfulness—were already sending out new branches eager to produce.

As he stretched out his hand above his head to grasp a cluster of the juicy purple orbs, he was arrested by the sight of his own hands. Brown and slightly callused from constantly tugging on Marcus's rope, nails caked with dirt, his hands looked at last like those of a shepherd. He smiled wryly after studying them for a moment.

"But a true shepherd, I will never be!" he concluded with certainty, as he reached for more of the ripe fruit.

Already he looked forward to his return home and the silken sheets that awaited him. *Enough of this insane sleeping on the ground.* Maybe he meant that thought; maybe he was simply afraid of all the loneliness and sacrifice that would go with being a shepherd—one who would lay his life down to guide and protect his charges.

The Visitor

Suddenly, a shadow fell across his face as he lay on the ground savoring the delicious grapes. His heart pounding, the king shot to his feet to face the intruder.

But what he found made him laugh aloud.

There before him stood a willowy young girl in peasant dress, a corner of her coarse brown skirt tucked up under her belt to free her feet to climb the hillside.

"So, you think I'm funny, do you?"

Shading her face with her hand so as to see clearly the interloper's face, she spoke again. "Shall I call my brothers to help me deal with you, thief that you are?"

Her voice is like music even when she is angry! the monarch thought as he looked intently into her face, ignoring her threat and captivated by the beauty that matched the voice. She quickly pulled her veil across her face and averted her own eyes from his.

He regained his voice and spoke politely, trying to put her at ease so she wouldn't go away. "Please don't call your brothers. I am not a thief—merely a traveler who much admires your beautiful vineyard."

Turning his gaze to the hillside and the neatly clipped rows, he added, "It must take an enormous amount of work to tend these properly." Then looking into her eyes, he asked, "Are these your vines and do you tend them alone?"

It was her turn to laugh. Solomon couldn't decide if her laughter sounded like water dancing over the rocks in a brook or like reed chimes in the wind. All that was certain was that he was smitten by everything about her from her sun-streaked brown hair—that insisted on straying out from under her scarf in a most provocative fashion—to her tiny waist and the delicate, tanned feet sandaled beneath the nondescript skirt. Her lithe figure, silhouetted against the morning sun, was as graceful as any deer he had seen upon the mountains to the west of Jerusalem as a child.

"No, these vines are not mine...though I wish they were," she sighed. "They belong to King Solomon. My brothers and I tend them while my little sister stays at home to help my mother."

"And your father?" Solomon asked gently, not wanting to pry. "Does he not help you?"

Her head fell forward slightly and she was silent for a moment. Then raising it again slowly, she responded with emotion in her voice, "He died last year at this time. He fell while chasing the foxes away from the vines and never recovered. It is difficult without him." Then, regaining her composure, "But Jehovah helps us. He is our strength and our joy." She let her veil droop without thinking, and Solomon glimpsed a most beautiful, easy smile.

"And who are you?" she inquired curiously, turning the attention deftly away from herself to him.

"No one special. A shepherd minus his sheep," he added with a smile, looking deep into her eyes. "I left them with a companion a few miles back," he waved evasively in the general direction from which he had come. His conscience felt a twinge at the lie. *But isn't this all a fantasy, this trip of mine?* With that rationalization, he dismissed the feelings of guilt.

She studied him for a moment then decided to believe him.

And so began the conversation. Because she had much work to do, he offered to help her if she would teach him about vine dressing as they went.

That she did. But after the hours of trimming and tying up branches and listening to quaint stories she told him of family, all he would remember was the melodious tone of her voice and the depth of beauty and tenderness he saw in her eyes. Her smile made his heart dance! He found himself memorizing her every move and every nuance of her mood throughout the day he hoped would never end.

They shared his provisions at high noon in the shade of the vines, and quenched their thirst at mid-afternoon from the stream that wound its way along the base of the hillside.

She invited him to her home in the nearby village of Shunam for supper, but he declined. He needed time alone to process what was happening and wasn't up to being interrogated by her brothers and mother. But he promised to be there again in the morning. She, in turn, promised to restock his provisions depleted by their noontime feast.

The lovely maiden left him in late afternoon beside the stream. Exhausted from all the climbing about the hillside, Solomon stretched out on the soft grass that felt like Heaven to him after the rocks of the desert of the last three days. He wanted to relive all he had felt that day toward this fascinating, yet simple, young woman...so much the "good Jewish girl" he had longed for since discussing the matter with Simeon a mere week earlier. The empty space in his heart was being filled with her presence.

Soon overcome by fatigue, the handsome son of David fell asleep in the shade of the vines...and dreamed of his Shulamite Lady.

Chapter Nine

Love Arrives

◦──〜──◦

She returned to him the next day at the first light of
dawn, and the sight of her took his breath away. Her
veil hung free, revealing a maiden of exquisite beauty—a
true daughter of Abraham. The way she moved reminded
him of the graceful lilies that bloomed and swayed gently in
the breezes within the palace courtyard back in Jerusalem;
the mystery in her eyes reminded him of the heights of Mt.
Hermon where the snow remained in the heat of summer.

He had not expected her so early and had not yet
refreshed himself at the stream. The usually impeccably
groomed king felt horribly grungy and unprepared to greet
the enchanting lady of the day before.

"You're here!" she exclaimed with a lilt to her voice as
she came upon the spot where she had left him the afternoon before.

Noting the remains of his campfire and his gray-brown
reed mat still spread upon the ground, she commented in
mock consternation, "I see you've made yourself right at
home in the king's vineyard." With her hands on her hips
and her lips pursed, she shook her head disapprovingly.
"What *shall* we do with you?" she asked, eyebrows raised,
concern in her eyes.

By then, Solomon was on his feet scrambling to gather
his provisions and stow them in the leather pouches that he

quickly slung over Marcus's waiting back. But he didn't grab the shepherd's coat in time.

"And even more importantly, what shall we do with *this*?" She gingerly picked up his sheepskin coat, feigning great annoyance at its odor. "Whew! Do you really wear this?"

His face turned crimson as embarrassment swept over him.

"Please forgive me. You caught me by surprise!" he blurted out as he snatched the coat from her outstretched hand and tried to hide it behind his back. Then, making an awkward attempt at hospitality, he offered, "Sit here for just a moment. I'll be right back."

As he threw the coat on the back of his donkey with one hand and rummaged in the nearest pouch for a fresh tunic with his other hand, she called after him, "You keep a king's hours! I thought you said you were a shepherd!" She clucked her tongue in remonstrance while a smile began to spread across her face. Solomon, however, didn't see the smile because his back was to her as he was hurrying to the stream to wash his face and change his clothes.

She must think I'm an idiot! This is not going well at all. He splashed the cold, clear stream water onto his face and arms, then vigorously dried them with his tunic of yesterday. Quickly, then, he slipped the fresh one on over his head and belted it snugly around his trim waist. Wetting his fingers in the stream once again, he ran them through his thick, dark hair and beard, bringing order to them both.

Drawing a deep breath to regain his composure, he turned to head back to the campsite with only one question in mind: "Will she still be there after this horrible beginning?" His heart nearly stopped beating at the thought of her having vanished. He tried not to run.

But there she was—resting casually on his mat, studying the horizon in the distance and lost in thought, her annoyance having seemingly vaporized. With great relief, he realized that she had just been making sport of him to ease her own entrance.

He grabbed the chance to move the focus away from himself and onto something neutral while getting a fresh grip on the situation.

"It's going to be a beautiful day, don't you think?" he called to her while stashing yesterday's shirt into his saddlebag.

This brought her back to the present. Flashing him an easy smile, she nodded affirmatively. "Beautiful, yes!" and then sighing, she added, "and therefore, busy!" She reluctantly rose to her feet, while her eyes kept searching his face.

"Why did you come here?" she probed gently and unexpectedly. "You are no shepherd, I suspect."

Rather than continue pretenses—but determined not to reveal his true identity for fear she would respond as to a king and not a man—he replied carefully. "I'm searching for something that calls to me from deep within my being, something that haunts me and will give me no rest until I find it." At that he knelt to the ground and he idly drew circles in a sandy spot.

Sensing he had more to say, she waited without a word, her eyes still fixed on his countenance, trying to read his heart.

"I keep going in circles—trying to do all God asks of me and trying to please the people who depend upon me, yet feeling as though my heart is held in the balance between joy and despair, hope and futility." He turned back to her, returning her probing gaze, but with a touch of "oldness" that she couldn't fathom.

"And have you found…love?" she hesitantly asked so quietly that he had to strain to hear the question.

"Love? Perhaps," he ventured, brushing the sand from his fingers and rising to face her fully.

"Yes," he corrected himself. "I *have* found love." He swallowed hard. Then slipping into a freedom he had never before allowed himself, he made his declaration without the slightest restraint. "Deborah, I have fallen in love with *you*."

Her eyes widened and she caught her breath.

It was her turn to speak. "I dreamed of you last night," she began hesitantly, "that you would say this," her voice invaded his spirit like a healing balm. Then gaining courage, she confessed, "I dreamed that we were then married in my village, but that one night I couldn't find you…that you were missing from my bed. I searched and searched for you without success." Uninterrupted by the shocked and silent Solomon, she continued her story.

"The village watchmen treated me cruelly for being about the streets in the middle of the night, and I returned, shamed." He gasped at such a thought, but she went on. "I awoke in tears, but then managed to sleep again when I realized that it was just a dream and that I would see you in the morning here in the vineyard.

"But a second dream came, as bad as the first!" she admitted in frustration. "You came home late, and I wouldn't let you in because I didn't want to bother getting out of bed to lift the latch!" she shook her head in disbelief at her own insensitivity, even in a dream. Her eyes saddened and filled with tears, one tear falling upon the front of her linen blouse.

She then slowly reached out her arms to him across the small space that physically separated them, beckoning him to come. "I would never reject you if you were mine. Never!" she whispered intently.

With a sense that time was standing still, they embraced there, the morning sun washing over them. He held her gently as though embracing a delicate dream that would vanish if he grasped too tightly. Tenderly, with his right hand under her chin, he tilted her face up to his. In the next moment their lips met in a kiss that held all the hope and hunger of two hearts that had sought eagerly for each other and now celebrated the end of that quest.

That Night

How long he had held her in his arms, how long the kiss had lasted, how short the day had been as they had shared their hearts and planned the future together—he could not measure as he lay under the stars that night. He would leave in the morning for Jerusalem and then return to claim her for his bride.

"Will the sun never rise?" the sleepless monarch complained at the moon that persisted in dominating the night sky. In his hand he held the piece of ribbon from her hair that she had left with him as a promise.

The Next Morning

"Hello, stranger!" the greeting broke into his dreams and brought him back to reality.

"Hello, yourself!" he returned as cheerily as possible given his groggy state from having been deep in sleep all night.

Approaching Solomon's campsite from the upper regions of the terraced hillside was a robust man, about thirty years of age, wielding a bow and sporting a string of foxes on a hemp rope, freshly caught that morning. He could only surmise that this man was one of Deborah's brothers.

Solomon, straightening up and getting his bearings, cast an admiring glance on the captured prey.

"Having a good morning's hunt, are you?" he asked good-naturedly.

Ignoring the question, the fellow dropped his catch on a patch of grass, while keeping a grip on his bow.

"You met my sister yesterday," he stated flatly. He eyed the erstwhile shepherd suspiciously. "She was quite taken with you."

Solomon smiled and relaxed a bit.

"But I am here to tell you that any hope you may have for her to be yours will never be realized...for she is engaged to another." Then, to make sure Solomon got the message, he added, "Her pledge has been given to the rabbi's son and they will marry next spring."

"How can that be?" Solomon whispered, his mouth suddenly dry and his thoughts thoroughly confused. The brother continued giving his speech.

"She enjoyed your help tending the vineyard, but will not be coming to see you today as planned," he stated without emotion. "Here are the provisions as promised to replenish yours, which you shared with her at noonday."

After placing them at Solomon's feet, he picked up the string of foxes and turned on his heels, heading abruptly for Shunam in the valley below. The king stood stock-still and stunned as though stricken from behind by an unexpected assailant.

Then, gathering his wits, Solomon reached into his saddlebags to produce the provisions she had already returned, proving that the brother had made a terrible mistake. But, to his shock, there were no provisions, no proof that yesterday existed.

The wide, confident stride of Deborah's brother halted briefly as he called back over his shoulder, "I'd suggest you leave at once and never come back." Then he resumed his trek away from the broken king left standing alone by the cold ashes of his campfire.

How can this be? His thoughts tore at him. *She told me that she was free, that she had been waiting all her life for me!*

He stood transfixed in his confusion...until slowly, the truth dawned upon him. Horrified, he soundlessly mouthed the words, *I must have dreamed the second day with Deborah! It never happened!* He shook his head in disbelief. *I arrived here just yesterday, apparently.*

Then to the sky, in desperation, he whispered his ultimate fear. "There were no declarations of love, no embrace, no sharing heart-to-heart about our future together. It was all just a wonderful, glorious dream!"

He slowly opened the still-closed hand that had been clutching the ribbon throughout the night. His hand was empty.

The dream had become a nightmare...and he felt like screaming.

CHAPTER TEN

BACK TO REALITY

Numb in heart and soul, Solomon staggered off into the brush as the bearer of the bad news disappeared into the valley below. The desolate king slumped to the ground, unmindful of the sharp rocks and prickly brush that poked at his legs and scratched his arms.

Hope that had risen so high, had fallen so low in the bare space of a moment—the moment of truth flashed by as if an illusion. But it was no illusion. It was fact. Deborah was promised to another and he would never see her again.

"Nothing matters anymore," he muttered to the sand beneath him. His heart—broken and disillusioned—was set adrift once more as the anchor he had cast into the dream broke loose and dragged listlessly along the bottom of his soul.

"What good is love?" he asked himself bitterly. "Full of promises, empty of fulfillment—it mocks me!

"I have been a fool this once, but I will not be a fool again!" he vowed angrily. Slowly and resolutely, he declared, "My heart will remain mine; never again will I give it to another." Then, egged on by his hurt and anger, he clarified his resolve. "I will capture every heart I can in the time I have left on this miserable earth. I will collect them as trinkets on a chain. But I will never love like this again."

Going Home

With the strength gained from his vow, he rose to his full height—brushing sand and prickers from his clothes, hands, and legs. He glanced absently at the small cuts on his legs inflicted by the rocks, and turned to pack Marcus and begin the solitary trek home.

"Well, this was a fool's journey from the beginning, wasn't it, my friend?" he spoke softly to the beast. He took a moment to rub the donkey's forehead affectionately before slipping the leather harness over his ears and tossing the reins onto his back.

"This day, I will ride. Enough of trudging like a peasant," he sighed. And for the first time, he thought about the request he had made of Jehovah early in his reign: "Grant me wisdom..."

"If only I had asked *instead* for the true love of a good Jewish girl like Simeon's Anna. Then I'd have been peacefully at home with my children, not plotting this ill-fated adventure," he concluded, kicking Marcus in the ribs to urge him forward.

The sky suddenly darkened and the thunder rolled in the distance. As it quickly drew his attention away from his useless ruminations, lightning streaked straight to the ground not a hundred yards in front of him!

The Warning

As the thunder rumbled ominously all around him and the lightning danced erratically behind the dark clouds overhead, Promise Giver spoke in the voice of the storm that had quickly taken possession of the hillside and the desert beyond.

Never, my son, never despise the Gift! You are ignorant of what you speak! Do you think it just knowledge or discernment...a smart decision, an insightful call amidst conflict?

Out of the storm, the Voice was in the thunder that rolled overhead. *Wisdom is greater than the universe and called forth life before the beginning of time. Wisdom is the source of a love far higher than that which you could have for any woman—even the fair maiden from Shunam. Wisdom will one day set mankind free from the tyranny of the selfishness and heartache from which even you suffer.*

Lightning flashed so close by, the eyes of the despairing king were blinded for a moment—a moment during which the Presence spoke once more.

You have seen but the shadow of the promise in the measure of wisdom that you were given!

Alone Again

As quickly as they had come, the Presence and the power within the storm were gone. Solomon found himself drenched not in rain, but in sweat, from the divine encounter. It was as though his very soul had been drawn into a wrestling match with God, from which—only by some stroke of mercy—he had been released before his demise.

As cool breezes began to rise and blow over him—sending a chill through his dampened body—the king slid from the back of his donkey and onto the ground. Dropping the reins and covering his face with his trembling hands, the exhausted king wept in self-pity. A tangle of emotions fought for control of his heart.

"What good is it if I can't figure wisdom out?" he shouted at the sky. "Why is what matters most so elusive?" He thought of his father's love for Jehovah, Simeon's delight in his wife, and Moshe's devotion to his family. The confused and miserable king felt doomed to stand at the window looking in on joy, never able to enter.

From then on, he trudged dejectedly at the donkey's side—eating nothing, feeling nothing, drinking only water, and avoiding the company of every other soul on the long journey home.

He intentionally skirted Hebron and Kephirah, fearing that what he would encounter in either place—whether the Presence or the comfort of family—would be like salt rubbed into an open wound. His own emptiness would be his only balm. At least emptiness he could understand. There were no surprises hiding in it to strike him down.

Jerusalem

As he approached the city three days later, he was stunned by the sight that greeted him. The massive towers of the temple stood like great bulwarks gripping the heavens, their golden surfaces shining so brilliantly in the sun that he had to shield his eyes! Never had he seen it from this vantage point before.

Strangely, comfortingly, the Presence lightly wrapped him in a soft embrace, despite the reprimand within the storm two days earlier. His heart jumped in relief that Promise Giver still loved him and had not removed the Gift from him. Someday, perhaps he would understand the mystery within it. Someday...

But today, something snapped into place within him as he eyed the city.

"The walls are shabby and much too low!" he exclaimed with a start. "How could I have missed that fact?" he wondered, berating himself.

At once he became again the builder-king, the architect of monuments of stone.

"The walls must be reinforced and raised at once, and the building of the Queen's Palace will commence as soon as I can garner the materials!" he spoke with authority to Marcus, then winced at his choice of companions.

"Enough of donkeys as well!" he pronounced in an attempt to regain his dignity. "From now on, I travel in chariots fit for the king that I am." Then turning to the faithful donkey who had patiently shared his week's escapade, he whispered into Marcus's floppy ear, "No offense, old friend," and then patted his flank affectionately.

Back to Business

This he understood—building, fortifying, commandeering resources. And so he would order the walls strengthened by fresh stone and mortar and raised in height proportionate to the height of the new skyline of the city. He would also construct watchtowers at regular intervals all around the city's walls, so that approaching enemies could be identified and routed long before reaching the golden city.

And the queen would get her palace...one more exotic than she had ever had while growing up in Egypt.

As he neared the eastern gate, he spied a stable boy lounging about the entrance, hoping for employment.

"Hey, boy!" he called. "Come get this donkey and take it to the stable owner just inside the gate!" at which the boy came running. After retrieving the scraps of parchments Moshe had given him, on which he had journaled during his trip, he announced, "Tell the stable owner he may have whatever I have left strapped to the beast."

Solomon slipped a silver coin into the lad's hand, and then handed him the reins. The shiny coin brought a broad smile to the boy's face and invited an inquisitive look toward the unkempt traveler. However, the boy's curiosity was soon overcome by his delight in being so handsomely paid for his services. He eagerly led the tired Marcus in through the gate and out of sight.

The weary, hungry king then walked a bit unsteadily along the perimeter of the city until he reached the springs that fed the aqueducts. Finding his old escape passage, he reversed the route and returned to the palace undetected.

In his chambers, he quickly peeled off the dirty shepherd's garments and set fire to them in his fireplace...all except the sheepskin coat, which he had intentionally left tied to the donkey's back. That, the stable owner could keep. After a leisurely soak in his garden bathing pool, he dressed for bed and then summoned a steward to bring him a meal of fruit and honey before retiring.

Never had grapes, pomegranates, dates, and nuts been so refreshing! "I'll have to do without more often just to experience this pleasure," he declared, smacking his lips with satisfaction when the meal was finished.

"And now, to bed," he sighed and yawned. "This too, I suspect, will be a new delight." He was right. He slept like a baby in his mother's arms.

But near sunrise, those arms belonged to another...the fair maiden of his vineyards. When he awoke, his heart ached unbearably. There would be no consolation for his loss, no remedy for his sorrow, unless...

An incredible plan began to form in his mind and grip his imagination.

———————

Traeh drooled as he watched with fascination the workings of the desperate king's heart. "Just like his father in so many ways," he spat gleefully, slime dripping from the corners of his crooked jaws. Turning to the demons who danced at his side, he slowly hissed, "I could not have devised a better plan myself."

CHAPTER ELEVEN

THE REVELATION

E arly the next day, after his morning prayers, Solomon dressed again in kingly attire—a long, flowing, gold-embroidered linen robe covering a soft, knee-length tunic with matching embroidery around the neckline, cinched at the waist by a braided purple belt. His first duty was to summon his advisors.

Shocked at his sun-browned appearance and the unconcealed and curious scratches on the king's legs and ankles, his advisors missed most of his report on the territory he had visited. All they could do was wonder at the nature of his adventure. He obviously hadn't rested!

But he was back, safe and sound. A collective sigh of relief was the wordless benediction upon the brief meeting.

Just before exiting, one of the men—who served as the court administrator—presented the king with the roster of cases awaiting his ruling.

"Are you ready, my king, to hold court today?" the rather rotund Micah asked as he bowed respectfully.

Expecting an answer to the affirmative—considering the fact that he had held clamoring clients at bay for a whole week already—Micah was dismayed when Solomon shook his head.

"One more day, Micah, I need one more day. I must work on my blueprints for the palace construction—especially of the judgment halls within it—and I must record my findings from this trip. I promise to resume court tomorrow morning." Seeing the disappointed look on his patient administrator's countenance, Solomon added quickly, "But I'll hear cases all day tomorrow—not just in the morning—to make up for the delay." Placing his hand reassuringly on Micah's shoulder, Solomon thanked him for all his hard work during the king's absence.

Micah's face brightened slightly at the words of affirmation. "Very well, my king. I will prepare the docket for tomorrow." Then bowing, he added, I trust your day will be a fruitful one." He resumed his exit from the hall and scurried to his own business quarters where he would attempt to bring order to the backlogged schedule.

Another Guest

As the rest of the men filed out, another figure appeared in the pillared doorway. Slender, stooped, and with coarse gray hair falling to his shoulders—but with keen eyes that missed nothing—Nathan the prophet bowed and requested an audience with the king.

Nathan had originally planned to simply pray with the king and apprise him of the joy with which the people were worshiping at the Dwelling, so recently completed. He had come bearing only good news and blessing.

But once in Solomon's presence, the seasoned prophet sensed that something was amiss. The king was changed somehow—no, *affected* somehow. There was a mixture of hope and desperation that Nathan had never witnessed about the king before.

"Come in, Nathan, come in!" Solomon warmly greeted him and motioned that he join the king in the inner chamber where they could have more privacy. "I'm so glad to see you!"

Indeed, he was. Nathan was his most palpable link to his mother and father and the secure world of his youth. He was also the one advisor with whom Solomon was always inexplicably vulnerable. Nathan's mere presence seemed to bind him to truthfulness.

After exchanging pleasantries, Nathan abbreviated his report and turned the conversation to the king's recent journey, surmising that the intriguing change originated there.

"So," he began after a moment's hesitation in which the prophet searched the young man's eyes in an attempt to probe his heart, "What did your trip uncover?"

Before Solomon could think to censor his response, he burst out with undisguised joy and yearning, "I found my true love, Nathan—a daughter of our people who makes my heart dance and every burden of life fall away!"

At this, the king sprang to his feet and began pacing in front of the old man, seemingly looking off into the future with longing.

"Her name is Deborah." The name fell from his lips like a song.

Nathan proceeded slowly, uncertain where this revelation would lead. "And did you bring her back with you?" he asked.

The handsome youth's face clouded over even as he continued pacing. "Not yet, but I will when the time is right."

Nathan reached out and touched Solomon's arm as he made a pass before him, hoping to arrest his pacing. "What about Jehovah's words to Israel that her kings must not multiply wives?" he asked seriously.

"Now don't start that!" the king shot back, obviously irritated, pulling away from the prophet's touch. Then regaining control of his emotions, he reasoned, "My father had several wives and no one complained. Why should the rules change for me?"

Nathan had no answer for the king other than the practicality of having undivided loyalty and avoiding the obvious pain of estranged children when one wife is favored over another.

"Of course, one wife is best," the king conceded, "but Jehovah has never struck any man down for having more than one, has He?" Again Nathan had no convicting response.

Deciding to change the direction of the dialogue, Nathan asked, "So where does Deborah live, and how does *she* feel about marrying you?"

The first part of the question was easy to answer. "In Shunam, in the hill country of Ephraim...a beautiful place." Solomon's memory of the vineyards and the valley below were so vivid and close to his heart that it seemed he must still be there.

Then to gain a moment more to frame the second part of his answer, he returned a question for a question. "Have you ever been to the vineyards of Shunam, Nathan?"

"Once or twice, I believe." But not to be distracted, the prophet asked again, "So how does she feel about your plan?"

"Ummm...she doesn't know my intentions yet."

"Is she *free* to marry you?" Nathan pressed on, sensing there was more to the story.

The probe Solomon had been dreading was out and had to be answered.

He began carefully, "She is promised to another," he conceded, "but I am convinced that her heart is with *me!*" he concluded emphatically.

Nathan's own heart ached at the dear boy's obvious dilemma that surely would have no joyous resolution.

"She doesn't know that I am the king, Nathan! She thinks I am a shepherd!" he laughed. Then soberly, unable to keep his scheme from Nathan—and desperately wanting his blessing—he confessed, "I will return to her within the month *as king* and simply take her for my own." And then, looking for all the world like the child whom his parents could never deny anything he desired, Solomon declared, "I'm the king! What I deem indispensable to my life and comfort cannot be kept from me!"

Then suddenly, out of a place in his heart that neither knew existed, the distraught king shouted, *"I will kill*, if necessary, to gain this woman!"

The malevolent declaration hung in the air around them, rendering them both speechless, casting a pall over the entire chamber. In the next instant, Nathan was on his feet and standing eye to eye with the young man whom he loved nearly as much as he had loved his father before him.

"Sit down, Son," Nathan finally urged calmly, his voice cutting a path through the desperation. "There is a story you must hear," he insisted.

Solomon, dazed and obedient, sat down beside Nathan on the brocade coach in the middle of the room and tried to listen.

The Story

"Once upon a time, there was a king—a wonderful and brave king whom all the people loved, who was deeply devoted to Jehovah."

Solomon sat silently, his gaze absently fixed on the tapestry that hung on the wall across from them, and his fingers fidgeting in his lap.

"This beloved monarch had several wives gained through battles won and was seemingly content. But not one of these women had truly captured his heart," he continued, finally catching Solomon's attention.

"Then one sultry evening, when the air was oppressively hot and he couldn't sleep, the king went to the palace rooftop seeking fresh air and relief."

Solomon turned and eyed him quizzically as though to say, "So where are you going with this?"

Nathan steadily pressed on, ignoring the look. "Across the courtyard, in the moonlight, the king saw a maiden—beautiful and as graceful as a doe—bathing on another rooftop. He was smitten with love and desire for her."

Now Solomon's curiosity was piqued and he began listening with great interest in spite of himself.

"So, because he was the king, he sent for her without regard for whether or not she was married already..." he continued, casting a sideways glance at Solomon. "She came, of course, because no one denies a king—and they spent the night together. Before dawn, she returned home."

Solomon interrupted at this point. "So what does this have to do with me?"

"Just listen. You'll see," the old man cleared his throat and again picked up the threads of his story.

"Before long, she sent word to the king that she was carrying his child, a fact of which she was certain because her husband had been off fighting for the king for many, many months. Not once had she and he slept together during that time.

"Upon hearing the news, the guilty king panicked and devised a scheme to cover his sin. First, he ordered the husband home so that he would sleep with his wife. But once there, the loyal soldier would have none of that. He declared that as long as his comrades were sleeping on the ground on the battlefield, he would not take comfort at home—so he spent the night on the ground outside the king's palace and would not go to his wife.

"Next, the king ordered the husband sent to a vulnerable position at the front line where he would surely be killed. Then the king could take her for his own wife."

"My God!" whispered Solomon. "He became a murderer, didn't he?"

"Yes, Son...and a thief."

"Did anyone ever know about it?" the young king asked.

"I'm afraid everyone did, and the beloved king became the laughingstock of many nations because of his hypocrisy."

With knit brows and a hint of fear in his voice, the young king hesitantly asked, "Who was this king, Nathan? Tell me!"

Putting his hand upon Solomon's shoulder as though to steady him, Nathan replied gently, "Your father."

Stunned, Solomon tried to process this information about his precious parent. He had two remaining questions, which he anxiously asked: "Was the woman my mother?"

"Yes," Nathan replied.

"And am I the child that brought such bloodshed?"

"No, Son. That child died."

"I see," Solomon responded, with a sigh of relief.

Nathan continued, "Please understand that your father repented deeply and thoroughly for his sin and returned wholeheartedly to Jehovah. God forgave him and gave him another son—you, Solomon—with the promise that this son would succeed him on the throne and build the temple that he was not allowed to build because of the blood on his hands. That very place of worship, which was your father's greatest dream, now stands on Mt. Moriah because you have faithfully done as he desired."

"Back to the story," the king insisted, ignoring the compliment. "Did all go well after Father repented?"

"I'm afraid not. God told him that his sons would be rebellious and bring him shame—which they did when they took their turns trying to wrest the kingdom from him for years to come. The repercussions of his sin—although he personally had been forgiven and blessed with you as a son—hung as a cloud over the rest of his reign and nipped at his heels like a hungry wolf seeking its prey."

"Was his knowing that he had set up his sons for rebellion because he sinned the reason he would never discipline them?" asked the king, remembering how helpless his powerful father had always seemed in the presence of his step-brothers' insolence. That had always puzzled him.

"Most likely," the prophet replied.

Neither spoke for the next few minutes.

"And what of my mother? Did she grieve the loss of her first husband?" he almost feared asking.

"She grieved deeply, Son, even though she loved your father. And to compound her grief, she forever feared that it had all been her fault somehow," Nathan shook his head sadly. "Women are sometimes like that, you know, even when they are not necessarily to blame."

Scenes of his mother in tears when he was a child—seemingly without reason or consolation—flooded his senses. Suddenly, the thought of Deborah bearing the guilt and shame for breaking her word to her fiancé in order to be with him—and perhaps even the regret she might come to experience, no matter how strong their love—was almost more than he could bear. To see her suffer would undo him.

Solomon rose wearily from the couch and walked to the open window. He stared vacantly straight ahead, his hands hanging limply at his sides.

"Please go now," he spoke barely above a whisper.

The old man hesitated, then silently left the chamber.

CHAPTER TWELVE

THE DECISION

❧

Alone, he wept. Tears fell for his parents' pain, but even more for his own.

He was caught—trapped within his very love for Deborah and the wisdom that inevitably gripped his soul. The thought of bringing her sorrow and shame immobilized him. And how could he run the risk of thwarting the mystic promise that was woven into the very fabric of his life and which held him safely in the arms of Jehovah? He knew that he would lose his very mind if he forsook his God.

Therefore, what recourse was left him?

The argument raged in his soul as his love for her burned white hot. The words he had penned upon rising that very morning cut like a knife:

Place me like a seal over your heart,
like a seal on your arm;
for love is as strong as death,
its jealousy unyielding as the grave.
It burns like blazing fire,
like a mighty flame.
Many waters cannot quench love;
rivers cannot wash it away.
If one were to give all the wealth of his house for love,
it would be utterly scorned.[10]

---

10. Song of Songs 8:6-7.

"Wouldn't such love overcome everything that might threaten its joy, every twist and turn of fate life dealt?" he asked himself aloud.

But there lurked in the recesses of his heart one fear—that Deborah's love for him was not as strong as his for her—that it would wither under the obstacles—or that she would be forever looking back over her shoulder to the man she had left behind. Sitting there alone in the chamber, his head in his hands, he tried sorting it all out.

I have assumed that her commitment to him is as mine to Adona—out of duty rather than true love. But do I know that for sure? he wondered, feeling more and more confused.

The memories of what had actually transpired between them that brief day in the hills of Ephraim persisted in mixing with those of his dream of their deep exchanges of heart and that unforgettable embrace. Rarely could he distinguish one from the other. The mental malaise threatened to drive him to distraction. If it were not for the scratches on his legs and the sun-browned face that looked back at him from his mirror, he'd wonder if the trip had occurred at all!

A cool breeze suddenly wafted through the open window, bathing him with the air his very soul needed to breathe. He drank of it in deep draughts, leaning toward the window to consume all of it at once so as not to perish. Within the cadence of that breath arrived the gentle Presence of Promise Giver.

Give her up, Solomon, whispered the Presence. **Give up the love that could drive you to desperation—even murder! Cling to Me and accept My love instead. Through this sorrow I will hide you in the shadow of My wings while your broken heart heals.** The thought of total surrender to Jehovah took Solomon's breath away.

After a long and difficult moment, Promise Giver probed his heart with the unspoken question: **Will you return for her?**

"No," the king resigned. Then stiffening his back and lifting his eyes defiantly, he added, "But I will never give my heart to another."

Obsessed

The king ate little for several days, but worked himself—and drove others—as if in a frenzy. Fortification of the walls commenced and the palace's foundation was laid within a fortnight. King Hiram again responded generously to his friend's request for materials such as gold, silver, cedar, and pine, and for craftsmen in return for corn, wine, and oil—commodities that were scarce in his island kingdom. Solomon also gave Hiram twenty cities situated in Galilee—which upon investigation, Hiram thought rather worthless. But their friendship was unimpaired by the unfortunate gifts and, indeed, grew over the years as Solomon's visits to his country and its temples—dedicated to pagan deities—increased.

As the palace walls rose, Solomon became more and more obsessed with the details of its appointments. He threw all his creative energy into designing beautiful and elaborate chambers for living and entertaining, exotic gardens, as well as awe-inspiring judgment halls for hearing court cases. In the main judgment hall, he erected a throne unlike any other in the world. This seat of justice was of hand-carved ivory atop six steps, each step with two lions at either end, and with two more beside the throne. The seat itself was carved into the body of a bullock, and all was held fast with gold.

The building, as a whole, was supported by quadrangular pillars of cedar and covered by a Corinthian-style roof. The walls within were of white, perfectly cut stone—the fourth row from the floor engraved with trees and plants with great leaves and spreading branches. He enlisted an artist to paint restful, pastoral scenes in luxurious colors on the plastered upper half of the walls. All but this exquisite artwork was covered with gold and silver.

Queen Adona's palace was soon called the *Forest of Lebanon*, named so for the stalwart and fragrant cedars of which it was constructed, harvested from the mountains of Lebanon northwest of Israel. The endless chambers therein were dazzling to behold.

Some of the living quarters were underground, but most were above ground and opened to the outdoors. Pathways from them led quickly into lush gardens filled with exotic and rare vegetation cultured by Solomon himself. All around the wondrous building were great shade trees and trellises laden with flowering vines—to protect those who passed that way from the heat of the day.

Although the gaunt and driven king meticulously planned every detail, from construction and appointments to precise protocol for the servants who would be assigned there for duty, his heart was not in it. The project was more a diversion—a desperate way to keep his heart from overtaking him.

Adona's Gift

On one particular night, Adona requested an audience with her constantly preoccupied husband. It was granted.

She met him in the anteroom to his bedchambers. Her beauty was inescapable. She was wearing a gossamer gown fragrant with the scent of lilies, and ribbons were interwoven through her long, shimmering black hair. He looked at her for the first time in months. She's grown up, he mused. Passion stirred within him—but strangely devoid of emotion. His heart seemed to be off somewhere else, unable to find its way back.

"I have a gift for you, my king," she said demurely. "It's a treasure I have had since I was a child, given to me by my mother." She reached within the folds of her gown and pulled out a golden, bejeweled box.

Holding it out to him from the opposite side of the room, she coaxed him to take it. "Come, Solomon. See what I have brought you!" *How charming she can be*, thought Solomon absently.

He advanced across the room toward her and the proffered gift. As he reached for the box, his curiosity rising, she moved toward him in response, slipping her free arm through his, drawing him close. "Promise me you will wear it always next to your heart," she murmured, stroking his cheek until he promised.

When he awoke in the morning, he found her still beside him. Her head lay upon his chest next to her gift, which was attached to a gold chain that encircled his neck. He slowly grasped the curious pendant and turned it over to see what was engraved upon it. The bust of Pharaoh, with a hooded cobra secured in his headpiece, stared back at him.

A cold chill ran down his spine. But he hadn't the energy to remove the strange amulet from around his neck. He fell back into an uneasy sleep from which he awoke with a start.

In his dream, the snake upon his chest was alive.

—————

Through the sinister talisman, Traeh's claws reached from hell and slowly sank into the vulnerable king's heart. "This will be easier than I thought," he smirked. "He will feel my grip till the day he dies..."

Part II

The Battle Rages

CHAPTER THIRTEEN

DRIVEN

E ach night by lamplight, the son of David wrote feverishly—compelled by the wisdom that brought resolution to others' conflicts yet created enormous conflict within his own heart. Truth inspired his pen. However, he remained an outsider looking through a window upon the life about which he wrote.

Solomon's favorite narrative form was the proverb—a brief, pithy saying that carried profound import. He had discovered the proverb in Arabia a few years earlier. The Hebrew proverbs he penned, often into the wee hours of the morning, spoke of wisdom and its benefits, the value of heeding instruction and correction, the necessity of integrity and faithfulness, and the dangers of infidelity and wanton love.

Whenever the stack of filled parchments grew high and threatened to tumble from his desk, he stopped writing long enough to group the writings by category and cover them carefully with embossed leather that had been cut to fit and stitched to hold the contents fast. The finished volume was subsequently added to the growing collection neatly arranged on carved cedar shelves in a special room in the palace. This room came to be called "The Wisdom Room" by those who frequented his home.

As the years passed, the wisdom literature of Solomon grew. Little did he know that his collection would constitute the largest in the world for generations to come.

He continued to write.

Unfortunately, while the truth he recorded fed his spirit and kept the Presence near, his vow to never love again yielded no resting place for the peace Jehovah offered him. His refusal to surrender the vow with which he shielded his heart from being broken instead kept it adrift and without solace.

But he could not see that.

Daytime Pursuits

His days were undeniably filled with governing or related affairs of state. Obsessed with building—perhaps because of his search for something new to satisfy his soul—he created imposing fortress cities: Hazor, Megiddo, and Gezer. These were situated to effectively protect the rest of his domain. Chief among those he hoped to deter was Hadad, leader of a rebel remnant of the Edomites whom David and Joab had subdued years before. Another was Rezon, ruler of Aram, who was Israel's adversary since Solomon's birth. Neither Hadad nor Rezon were any match for Israel's army, but they would be thorns in Solomon's side throughout his reign.

At the other end of the spectrum were the cities he developed for the sheer benefit of pleasure-seeking noblemen. Because of the temperate climates and abundant springs of these cities, travelers came from far and near to relax under the spreading palm trees by day and feast in the opulent dwellings by night. Wine and song, women and hopes of love abounded. Whether satisfied or not, seekers continued to pour into these cities. Frequently among them was the lonely king of Israel.

When he had exhausted land to develop within his own borders, he stretched his occupation far into the desert above Syria, building the great city of Tadmor. It was only two days' journey from Upper Syria, one day's journey from Euphrates, and six days' journey from Babylon. He also invaded and conquered the remaining Canaanite lands—stretching from Mt. Lebanon to Hamath—conscripting the inhabitants into forced labor or domestic slavery on his properties throughout the land. So began his practice of subjugation of one man to another.

Amidst all this activity, in every spare crack of time, he continued to immerse himself in the study of the religions and philosophies of the heathen peoples in the cultures around him—Phoenician, Hittite, Egyptian, Chinese, Indian, and Arabian—but very specifically that of each new wife he acquired. Pantheism, as well as the mythological gods and goddesses of many of these nations, made for especially uneasy bedfellows alongside Jehovah in the land of Israel. Often, the mystic amulet he wore around his neck burned into his heart...but he dismissed it in his preoccupation.

And all the while, the Gift dominated as he continued to hear cases in the Great Judgment Hall, ruling wisely day after day, despite the dissonance growing within him.

An Old Friend

One morning before leaving for court, a courier arrived with a letter for him written on a small papyrus scroll. He broke the seal and read:

Dear Solomon,

Can you find a few moments for an old friend? I miss you.

Sincerely,
Simeon

"Take this message back to the sender immediately," he instructed the courier, handing him a quickly written response. It read:

> *Simeon,*
>
> *Please meet me in the palace gardens tonight at twilight. Enter by the main corridor and a servant will bring you to me.*
>
> *Another old friend,*
> *Solomon*

As he watched the courier hurry away, he thought back to the last time he and Simeon had met. It was soon after the heartbreaking trip into the hill country of Ephraim where he had fallen in love with the one woman he could never have. Simeon had tried to comfort the king, but to no avail. The only thought-provoking sentiment Solomon had taken away from their time together was something his friend had said:

> *Trust in the Lord with all your heart*
> *and lean not on your own understanding;*
> *in all your ways acknowledge Him,*
> *and He will make your paths straight.*[11]

He could still recognize wisdom. Yet, however valuable he knew the advice to be, he could not find a way to appropriate it for himself. It found its place alongside so many other thoughts that had spoken truth to him but eluded his grasp—scrupulously recorded in one of his leather-bound volumes.

---

11. Proverbs 3:5-6.

The Visit

That evening was warm and comforting, as June evenings often are. The intoxicating fragrance of the garden flowers was adrift on every breeze.

"How I wish Anna and the children could see your garden!" Simeon exclaimed upon arriving, struck by the amazing array of vivid colors and the beauty of the environment.

"Bring them!" urged Solomon. "Come whenever you like," he encouraged his simply clad friend, as he guided the awestruck Simeon up one pathway and down another. "Nothing would give me more pleasure than to share this with you and your family.

"You know," Solomon wistfully added, "the love you share has been my inspiration for a very long time." A shade of melancholy invaded his voice as he continued, "Since I can't find such joy for myself, to celebrate yours would bring me a measure of comfort."

Their steps slowed and Simeon searched his friend's face. New wrinkles had stolen onto the king's chiseled features, forming vague patterns in his olive skin. An inexpressible sadness lay behind his eyes.

"Have you no happiness of your own, my friend?" Simeon asked gently, his tone soft and caring.

The king's pace suddenly quickened at the question, although he kept his eyes fixed upon the flowers that grew in profusion along the path.

"Oh," he sighed, "I have a king's happiness." Then matter-of-factly, he enumerated, "All is well in the territories I govern, the land prospers, and the people seem pleased with my leadership." Then brightening perceptively, he added, "I've even garnered quite an impressive stock of thoroughbred horses and handsome chariots—mostly gifts from other nation's rulers who want to curry my favor."

Simeon hadn't the courage to remind his dear friend of Jehovah's law admonishing kings against collecting, among other things, great numbers of horses for himself. Instead, he simply laughed aloud at this last revelation.

"Remember how you hated it when your father insisted that camels and donkeys were the best way for kings to get about in this part of the world? And how badly you wanted to ride in chariots instead, drawn by magnificent horses just as the Egyptians did?"

The king chimed in, "As a child, I *dreamed* of chariots almost every night. When awake, I drew hundreds of pictures of them—all sorts of sizes and shapes." Slapping Simeon on the back, he laughed as he announced, "And now I own far more than my dreams could ever contain!"

"I daresay, even more than Pharaoh himself!" rejoined Simeon.

After looking quickly over his shoulder, the king put his right forefinger to his pursed lips and said, "Shhhh. Don't let Adona hear you say that!"

They both broke out in peals of laughter.

But within seconds, the sadness, which had been for a moment driven away, returned to the king's face.

"There is little joy in having possessions without a family to enjoy them with," he concluded.

To which Simeon immediately responded, surprised by such a statement, "But you *have* family! You have...*how many* wives and children by now?"

Skirting the question, Solomon qualified his remark with concerted intensity. "Only love creates a family, Simeon, and I have none in my heart for these women. They represent conquests, treaties, and political arrangements...and sometimes sheer impulse on my part, of which

I am not proud." He turned his gaze to the sky and shook his head.

After drawing a deep breath and exhaling slowly, he explained simply, "One is as a thousand others. My heart remains out of reach, no matter how hard I try to rally it for more than physical passion."

Visibly regrouping, Solomon shifted the conversation—and their stroll—onto another pathway.

"Come! I want you to see my latest addition." Like a child, the silk-gowned and elegant king sprinted toward another section of the gardens as though running from the previous question. Simeon hustled to keep up with him.

There, in an open, grassy area, strutted five indigo and turquoise male peacocks. Upon the human intrusion, the birds spread their tail feathers into fans—rendering them each nearly five feet in height and quite imposing. At the very same time, they let loose a most disconcerting, shrill noise—a cross between the scream of a jungle cat and the honk of a goose—that literally pierced the night air and changed the mood of all within earshot.

Simeon had never witnessed such sights or sounds.

Especially haunting was the elliptical design clearly bound into the colors of each outspread plume—which looked to Simeon for all the world like a row of cold-blooded eyes watching his every move.

"What strange creatures!" was the only response the king's polite guest could muster at first. "I must confess that I'm not sure I like them very much. I prefer simple, understandable creatures such as donkeys and chickens," he nervously stated.

Seeing the puzzled look on Simeon's face, Solomon gave him more time to sort out his feelings.

Soon Simeon spoke again. "They are incredibly beautiful, but somehow not what they seem." Shaking his head, he concluded, "I don't think I can trust them not to attack me if I turn my back!" He laughed nervously.

"Well," Solomon quietly rejoined the conversation, "thanks for your honesty, my friend, although I'm a little hurt that you don't appreciate my new pets. I must admit, however, that you're right. They're really not very loyal, but rather out for themselves at every turn. I believe that if I didn't feed them, they'd eat me for dinner!"

The king continued more reflectively, "But what a study in contradiction they are! Mesmerizing yet menacing...they fascinate me..."

Turning to leave the area for the more peaceful one they had left a moment before, Solomon mused aloud, "I think they mean well and can't help themselves..."

Simeon had the distinct feeling that the king was no longer talking about the strange birds in the palace garden.

The Vision

Later that night, as the king tried in vain to embrace sleep, the Presence of Promise Giver bathed the room with a soft glow, driving back the darkness.

Solomon, My son, your heart is being weighed in the balances, and I fear for you. Go to the window and look up into the night sky. There is something you must see, coaxed the Presence gently.

Mystified but obedient, the sleepy king rose and slipped on his satin robe while stepping hesitantly toward the window in the eastern wall of his chamber. He pushed open the shutters, which moved easily upon well-oiled hinges, and cast his eyes to the sky.

What he saw was riveting...

In the cosmic expanse above, ponderous iron scales emerged, suspended between Heaven and earth, to weigh time to come. On one side, nestled in a gilded saucer hanging from massive links of chain, lay a child. On the other side, in a matching saucer, and perfectly balancing the child lay a gift wrapped in blazing color—crimson sparks shot from it into the sky in all directions.

Even as he was about to ask the identity of the child, he knew. He saw himself within the eyes of the infant stirring upon the scales.

Now, look at the child's heart, prompted Promise Giver. *What do you see?*

Solomon's eye was immediately drawn to an ever-widening fissure, clearly definable, wending its sinister way through the heart of the boy! At the sight of it, hair stood up on the king's arms and sweat suddenly dotted his forehead.

At that moment, another voice—that of the Dark Dragon, Traeh—pressed insistently against his soul. "It's nothing to worry about! Where is the danger in a tiny crack, a mere disparity, a shadow at best?" Traeh whispered. "Your heart is unique and distinctive, that is all. Its destiny is beyond that of common man, and the risk will be worth the treasure."

The voice strangely chilled him and warmed him at the same time. He dared to look more closely at the fissure forming in the child's heart. Flitting about within the deepening chasm were alternating and obscure images of prancing horses, golden treasures, and the veiled faces of a multitude of women beckoning to him seductively.

Suddenly, he could barely breathe, for the chamber behind him seemed to have had the very air sucked out of it.

In the next instant, from the Gift that had been glowing brightly in the balance opposite the child, a blazing ball of fire shot straight to the earth! Solomon held what little breath he could still summon, expecting a great conflagration as one city or another was consumed in flames—set ablaze by Jehovah's wrath.

But there was no sign of fire on the earth...and when he raised his head to examine once again the balance displayed in the heavens, it had disappeared! The sky was once again as black as ink, punctuated only by innocent stars.

Solomon instinctively wiped the perspiration from his face, as he had when he was a child. After shedding his robe, he poured cool, clean water from an ornate pitcher on his nightstand into its matching basin. Cupping his hands into the water, he splashed it several times upon his hot face, and then dried his face and hands with a linen towel. He smoothed his hair and took a deep breath. Soon all was as it had been.

He slipped into bed again, emotionally and mentally exhausted.

Then out of the stillness, Promise Giver's gentle voice urged, ***Give Me your heart, Son. Trust Me as your father did. All will yet be well.***

But Solomon just rolled over onto his side and pulled his feather pillow over his head.

———

Heaven and hell withdrew...and waited.

CHAPTER FOURTEEN

THE CHARIOT KING

_____

As Israel's boundaries expanded, so did Solomon's desire for adventure and acquisition. He was indeed an entrepreneur obsessed with organization and control.

Every city had levels of government, a strong military presence, thoroughly equipped stables housing hosts of chariots and charioteers—all closely monitored by the king himself. Order and protocol were the watchwords of the day, and everything was done on a massive scale. Nothing the king installed or instituted was less than impressive.

The King's Pleasure

Solomon's favorite pastime was riding through the countryside in one of his spectacular chariots surrounded by an entourage of chariots driven by the finest and most resplendent horsemen in the world. His horses—numbering about 22,000 and bred for their speed and beauty—were carefully groomed and exercised daily. His drivers were not only expert charioteers, but also tall, handsome young men with long, glistening hair. Before each outing, they were dressed in garments of Tyrian purple, and their heads were sprinkled with gold dust that sparkled when the sunlight touched it.

These chariots and drivers were on 24-hour call in the Chariot Cities—several major cities in Israel—ready in an instant for Solomon's amusement or that of one of his foreign friends. Of course, a handsome contingency was retained in Jerusalem for his daily early-morning rides. His chariot jaunts into the countryside were made more comfortable by the newly created roads—paved with crushed black stones—that emanated from the city in all directions.

Solomon's favorite destination was Etham, which lay about fifty miles from Jerusalem. This area abounded in lush gardens and gently flowing streams. There, he would pause for an hour or so to meditate and gather his thoughts for the day.

Maintaining all of this was immensely expensive, but the tributes and taxes that poured in—plus the labor costs that were saved by using vanquished people for all menial tasks—were sufficient to finance every whim of the king.

More

As the land was subdued, Solomon's eyes turned toward the sea. In rare moments of solitude in the royal garden, the king paced restlessly, imagining vast stores of treasures on faraway coasts. The fire that wealth had lit in the jagged crevasse in his heart burned insatiably.

Even though land-bound in Jerusalem, the king could smell the salt water and hear the shouts of the seamen as they sighted the land of a distant shore.

But I can't go there myself, he scowled as he paced. *I can only dream while others have the adventure*, he complained to himself.

"What's that country I hear the most about, my friend?" he queried a disinterested peacock that strutted within hearing distance. "Ah, India! I have heard from good sources that in the mines of India is the purest and most brilliant gold known in the world!" he continued to the peacock, waving his arms excitedly and trying to get the bird to share his enthusiasm. Instead, the strange creature arrogantly turned to strut away from the king, dismissing him with a piercing cry that destroyed the ambiance of the moment.

Solomon shook his head in disgust and turned back toward the palace. His dreaming was over. It was time for action.

He called a special session of his advisors to discuss the matter of sending an expedition by sea to India.

"By sea?" Micah asked incredulously. "We don't have any ships!" Out of respect for the king, he stifled the desire to laugh.

"Of course, we don't," Solomon answered indulgently. "But we can build them." He confidently strode to the closet at the end of the room from which he produced a large parchment. He carefully spread it out on the table where the men could see it. On it was a map showing the lands and seas between Israel and the intended destination.

"I've already contacted King Hiram, who has ships and crews aplenty, and he will be delighted to help us in our pursuit," he continued, purposely not looking anyone in the eye quite yet. He didn't want to give permission for an interruption. "For a reasonable fee, Hiram will send us his shipbuilders and materials, and our very own ships will be built!"

"What about navigators?" Barak piped up. "Our people know nothing about sailing on the open seas! Is Hiram going to provide those as well?" he asked skeptically.

"As a matter of fact, he will!" Solomon continued patiently. "His navigators and pilots will train our men during an actual voyage," the king concluded, obviously pleased with all the arrangements.

As usual, the men—who barely understood the ramifications of all this but were willing to trust their king's judgment—acquiesced. By the time the meeting adjourned, they were actually excited about the challenging enterprise themselves...all except Barak who looked askance upon the entire project.

"It will all work out," Solomon assured him as they left the chamber together.

And so, a new port for Israel's ships was developed in the Egyptian Bay at the south end of the Red Sea, in a place called Ezion-geber to accommodate the new venture. Hiram was true to his word, and all went as planned.

By the time a small fleet was ready to sail—Israel's pilots having been tutored for a season by Hiram's men on Sidonian ships first—King Solomon had a team of explorers equipped to penetrate the jungles and chart the hills of India. Their primary destination would be Ophir, where the finest gold was buried deep in the earth.

After two long years of suspense, the ships returned laden with not only 400 talents of gold, but also a strange new material called algumwood as well as precious stones. Solomon immediately incorporated the algumwood into the steps of the Dwelling and the Royal Palace. He also used it to make harps and lyres for the musicians who ministered in worship before Jehovah. Nothing like these instruments had ever before been seen in Israel.

After that initial voyage, the ships made regular trips to foreign ports from which they returned every three years with gold, silver, ivory, apes, and baboons. National pride soared as Israel's wealth increased daily.

The king seemed to have boundless energy and ingenuity. However, he slept little and increasingly drank strong wine to ease the desperation and loneliness that drove him. Only Nathan surmised the extent of his inner turmoil...the contradictions that roared in his soul.

At Night

When most restless, Solomon returned in his heart to the days of his childhood when his father could hold his world together with a song. In these moments of simplicity before God, the king composed beautiful proverbs by lamp-light—after others were asleep and serenity engulfed the palace. Embraced by the Presence, he shaped what he saw in the spirit into words and verse that would warn of danger and encourage justice and right living among his people.

About one's reputation, he wrote:

A good name is rather to be chosen than great riches,
and loving favor rather than silver and gold.[12]

About youth and discipline:

Train up a child in the way he should go,
and when he is old, he will not depart from it.[13]

About business matters:

The Lord abhors dishonest scales,
but accurate weights are His delight.[14]

About marriage:

A wife of noble character is her husband's crown,
but a disgraceful wife is like decay in his bones.
May your fountain be blessed,
and may you rejoice in the wife of your youth.[15]

---

12. Proverbs 22:1, KJV.
13. Proverbs 22:6, KJV.
14. Proverbs 11:1.
15. Proverbs 12:4; 5:18.

About avoiding sexual sin:

For the lips of an adulteress drip honey,
and her speech is smoother than oil;
but in the end she is bitter as gall,
sharp as a double-edged sword.[16]

About evil companions:

My son, do not go along with them,
do not set foot on their paths;
for their feet rush into sin,
they are swift to shed blood.[17]

About self-control:

Better a patient man than a warrior,
A man who controls his temper than one who takes a city.
A man of knowledge uses words with restraint,
and a man of understanding is even-tempered.[18]

About strong drink:

Wine is a mocker and beer a brawler;
whoever is led astray by them is not wise.[19]

About friendship:

A friend loves at all times,
and a brother is born for adversity.[20]

---

16. Proverbs 5:3-5.
17. Proverbs 1:15-16.
18. Proverbs 16:32; 17:27.
19. Proverbs 20:1.
20. Proverbs 17:17

About one's words:

> *He who guards his lips guards his life,*
> *but he who speaks rashly will come to ruin.*[21]

About trusting God:

> *The name of the Lord is a strong tower;*
> *the righteous run to it and are safe.*[22]

About taking advice:

> *Pride only breeds quarrels,*
> *but wisdom is found in those who take advice.*[23]

But when the lamplight was extinguished, the war again raged within. His own growing hypocrisy threatened to drive him mad.

One particular night during the harvest season, when the air was filled with the musty smell of ripe wheat and dried herbs, Solomon stole out of the palace as he often did and up to Mt. Moriah—to the Dwelling that shone in the moonlight. There, Promise Giver searched his heart and truth prevailed. There, he found his bearings again; there he climbed into the arms of his God and embraced the hope of the promised deliverer to come.

In a voice as soft as the autumn wind, Jehovah spoke into his spirit.

Son, let Me love you not only here, but during every other hour of the day or night. My love—if you will

---

21. Proverbs 13:3.
22. Proverbs 18:10.
23. Proverbs 13:10.

embrace it in each circumstance—will complete you and give you peace. I alone can bring together the areas of your heart that are drifting apart. But, He warned, *you must let go of the anger you carry over your losses.*

At those words, the poison of Solomon's bitterness churned in his soul, sending adrenaline throughout his body. He found it nearly impossible to sit still and listen, even though his life might well depend upon it. It suddenly felt as though invisible talons gripped his wounds, jerking him from emotion to contradictory emotion—never allowing him rest.

He cried out in his anguish, "I feel cursed! When Truth speaks—even through my own mouth and pen— cynicism and doubt tear at me from every angle!"

Falling to the cold stone floor before the brazen altar, he confessed his driving misery. "I write of trusting You, while I live in mortal fear of giving You control! I write of love, while I despise the very commitment that lies at its heart!" Then wearily he drew himself up to his knees, trying to regain his composure after such frightening transparency of heart.

Promise Giver's response was intense and urgent. *Then forgive, Solomon, forgive! Forgive Deborah for not being free to love you in return. And lay down your secret anger at Me for the rules that prevented your taking what didn't belong to you.*

This last statement struck a nerve in the agonizing king. It was true that he was angry at Jehovah, but to know that Jehovah could invade his soul and read its contents without his consent made him angrier still.

Promise Giver continued in spite of Solomon's reaction.

And now, repent of your insistence that you alone can know what is best for you. Repent of thinking that you can break My laws with impunity and remain above judgment for your sins. Even wisdom does not give you that right! the Voice thundered. *The Gift you received from Me can, in an instant, become inconsequential. It does not determine who you are...or release you from the responsibility that every man bears before Me.*

Then quietly, as though the storm had passed, Promise Giver gently probed, *Do you want to be free of the demon that drives you? Will you forgive others their choices and repent of trying to control your life on your own terms?*

Solomon struggled to his feet, visibly shaken.

The ultimate promise will come, Son, whether peacefully through your obedience, or in great distress brought on by your rebellion. The Messiah will come, Solomon, whether you die loved—leaving a secure kingdom in wise hands, or you die despised—leaving a divided and disillusioned kingdom in the hands of fools.

After a heavy silence, Promise Giver whispered the question that would haunt the king the rest of his days: *After dispensing wisdom to everyone else, will you not apply it to your own heart?*

Solomon wept bitterly...but would neither forgive nor repent.

Entrenched

Solomon trudged back to the palace with an ever-growing longing for Deborah that had turned fierce during the battle for his heart that night. No matter what delusions might yet spring from this addiction to her memory, he would let no one replace her—not even Jehovah.

Alone in his chambers at last—fatigue held at bay by obsession—he threw aside his robe and sandals, rolled up the sleeves of his tunic, and sat down at his writing desk.

As he pulled a fresh parchment scroll into place before him, a melancholic melody arrested him. He knew at once that this song lived in the fiber of his heart, the marrow of his bones.

Pen in hand, he sat motionless as the captivating tune wrapped itself around his heart and evoked images of the hills of Shunam—the dancing eyes and the whimsical beauty of the voice of the maiden who dwelt there. At one moment it soothed his raveled nerves and hinted at joy to come. At the next moment, it burned with a fire that frightened him. But no matter how dangerous it felt, he could not let it go.

"Perhaps," he anxiously whispered into the small circle of lamplight that illuminated the desk before him, "if I confine the haunting dream to parchment, it will find a resting place and the burning in my heart will ease."

And so he began to write the Song of Songs—a tale of the purest love a man and woman could know. The night hours flew by unnoticed as he wrote. Vibrantly, the Lover and his Beloved came to life on the scroll as the story unfolded—the enchanting courtship of a sweet country maiden and the love-struck king disguised as a shepherd.

Putting it in words upon parchment somehow settled it as a fairy tale out of someone else's imagination. A degree of rest began to settle into his soul.

The Final Blow

However, just as the sun crested the Judean Hills, an urgent knock came at his door. Quickly rolling up the scroll to be sealed later, he hurried to the door to see what the unusual interruption meant.

"Your Majesty," the guard breathlessly began, bowing at the waist in respect. "Nathan is ill and calls for you. Will you go to him?"

"Of course, at once!" the shocked king replied without a second's hesitation. But as he hastily donned his robe and sandals, horror swept his heart.

"Is he...dying?" the king asked as he followed the guard down the long corridor and through the courtyard toward Nathan's dwelling nearby.

"I don't know, Sir," was the careful reply. But from the grim look on his face, Solomon suspected the worst. Memories of his father's death, then his mother's, washed over him leaving him dizzy.

The guard, detecting his unsteadiness, took his arm saying, "Forgive me for taking the freedom..." The dazed king made no reply.

Just as they reached the home where Nathan kept quarters when he was in Jerusalem, the wail of the women within erupted. Almost immediately, a servant slipped from the house and whispered to the guard, "Don't trouble the king any further. The prophet is dead!"

Right there in the street, Traeh croaked into the stunned king's heart.

"What kind of God strips a man of his loved ones and still expects devotion?" croaked Traeh into the stunned king's heart. "Such devotion requires a blindness that is beneath you, Solomon," he chided.

"Only a man's wits can be trusted," the evil presence continued. "Only a man's power can bring comfort when all else human is gone." And then he laughed raucously, sending a shudder through Solomon's frame, and the air turned strangely cold around him as he stood there in the street.

CHAPTER FIFTEEN

THE VISITOR

King Solomon was never the same. While the intensity
of writing, studying, building, and ruling continued
unabated, the look in his eye changed. It reflected a fathomless void within his heart.

Simeon noticed it. "What is it, my friend?" he asked
one rare day when they had an hour to stroll in the palace
gardens.

"What is *what*?" the king absently replied, a little irritated at the attention.

"You look as though you have lost your best friend!"
he tried to say lightly.

"Oh? I suppose so. I have lost not one but four—counting
my Shulamite fantasy. All I have left is you," he answered
with heart-wrenching sadness.

Simeon studied the king's face. There was little color
in it, for he seldom went riding since Nathan's death. If he
wasn't holding court, he was feverishly writing, studying,
planning expansion, or entertaining foreign heads of state.

As they reentered the palace courtyard, a courier
arrived with a gold-embossed scroll sealed with the scarlet
seal of Ethiopia. "For you, Sire," the courier said, bowing
and handing him the scroll.

With but the slightest twinge of curiosity, Solomon broke
the seal and began to read the message aloud to his friend.

The Queen of Sheba wrote simply: *I have heard of your great wisdom and desire to witness it for myself. At your invitation, I will visit you in the spring.*

Simeon smiled. "Maybe this visit is just what you need, my friend."

The king appeared unmoved, but nodded obligingly. "It'll be an amusing diversion, I suppose."

At which Simeon quickly added, "The stories about her are of no small consequence. She'll be a very amazing guest, I daresay!"

Glancing at the sun as it moved lower in the sky, Simeon exclaimed, "I'm late for dinner!" He hastily bid the king good-bye and left him standing alone on the granite steps of the palace. Just as Simeon reached the street, he called back, "Enjoy the visit, my friend!"

In the Spring

She came...in all her splendor. She came to Jerusalem to test his wisdom with hard questions of both practical and philosophical natures and to see for herself if the legends about his sagacity and wealth were true. She arrived with a great caravan of camels carrying gifts and treasures to be given to the king at the end of her visit. Although at first disinterested, the king felt honored that she would be visiting him. He hoped that this noble woman from the distant land of Ethiopia would bring color to his gray world.

Servants specifically assigned to see to her comfort settled her into one of the guest suites in the palace. She rested for three days before requesting an audience with the renowned king of Israel.

On the Third Day

"Your Majesty, the Queen of Sheba awaits," the court attendant announced with solemnity to the king, who sat upon his great throne in the judgment hall.

"Usher her in at once!" he answered in his most dignified voice, a slight lump forming in his throat.

What will she be like? he wondered, having heard fascinating tales of her wealth and beauty.

The massive hand-carved and gold-covered cedar doors swung open soundlessly, revealing a stately woman of about thirty-five years of age. She was dressed in a flowing ivory-colored silken garment curiously decorated overall with swirling floral patterns created by precious stones of every color. Sparkling amethysts, rubies, sapphires, and emeralds encrusted the gown both front and back, extending even throughout the train that trailed elegantly in her wake. Silk sleeves of Tyrian purple complemented the ornate body of the garment. Woven into the long, shiny black hair that was piled high on her head were delicate feathers of an iridescent hue, reminding him of the shimmering peacocks in his garden.

When Solomon saw her that day for the first time, he was immediately entranced. Her sultry beauty took his breath away. Her flawless, dusky skin; her deep, mystical dark eyes; and her majestic bearing and light step gripped him. No woman he had ever met—except his Shulamite Lady—had been so mesmerizing. Here was not only a strikingly beautiful woman, but a stateswoman of obvious nobility as well.

About halfway across the room, she stopped and spoke. Her voice resonated with strength and confidence and brought him back to the purpose of this amazing occasion.

"King Solomon," she said in Hebrew to honor him, "it is a pleasure to at last be in your presence. I look forward to receiving your wise replies and insight to the difficult questions I bring from my country. May your wisdom prove to be all that it is reported to be."

At this, he stood and they both bowed in mutual respect. He then descended the steps that had elevated him above her and met her in the center of the room. As he drew closer, he marveled at her regal bearing.

"Let us adjourn to more comfortable quarters in the palace," he invited his intriguing guest, motioning toward a door adjacent to the one through which she had entered. The Queen's attendants deftly lifted her train and resettled it behind her as she turned to exit with her host.

Their Time Together

For several months, the Queen of Sheba questioned him to test his knowledge and ability to reason, watched him closely as he held court and settled disputes of every kind within his kingdom, and traveled with him all about his vast realm. She toured the model cities he had built and was witness to the extent of his control over not only his land, but also those that bordered it. She saw his great treasure stores, quarries, mines, and stables, and she was feted at every stop.

She enjoyed his horses the most; so whenever they were in Jerusalem, she accompanied him on his chariot ride into the country to the gardens at Etham.

"We have horses, too," she laughed on one of their rides. "Only they are white with black stripes!"

"And which way do the stripes run?" he asked in puzzlement, imagining that they ran horizontally from head to tail, making the beasts look for all the world like galloping fences.

"Why, vertically, of course! They encircle their necks and bellies." Then trying to imagine what he might have thought, she asked, "What did you think?" as she cocked her head playfully and looked at him curiously.

While he was undeniably drawn to her and they shared an easy camaraderie, something in her bearing kept him at arm's length. Perhaps she herself was too wise, too wealthy—too much like himself—for him to feel comfortable pursuing her romantically. For whatever reason, although their attachment continued to grow on an intellectual level, they both avoided the entanglement of love. Finally, Solomon had met a woman who challenged him. It was exhilarating for them both, but never bound them at the heart.

When it came time for her to return to her country, they met once again in the judgment hall where he sat in state upon the massive throne that dwarfed all else in the room.

She was, in turn, adorned as she had been upon her arrival. As her beauty struck him afresh, he wondered, *How could I not have fallen in love with her?* But he hadn't, and she was leaving.

Again her confident, clear voice captured his attention.

She began simply, "The report I heard in my own country about your achievements and your wisdom is true! But I did not believe what they said until I came and saw with my own eyes. Indeed, not even half the greatness of your wisdom was told me; you have far exceeded the report I heard."

In sincerity, she exclaimed, "How happy your men must be! How happy your officials, who continually stand before you and hear your wisdom! Praise be to the Lord your God, who has delighted in you and placed you on His throne as king to rule for the Lord your God. Because of the love of your God for Israel and His desire to uphold them forever, He has made you king over them, to maintain justice and righteousness."

After a brief pause, she concluded by saying, "Please accept these humble gifts from one who has witnessed with gratitude your wisdom." Turning slightly to her right, with a wave of her hand, she signaled to her servants to enter with her gifts for the King. When they had finished depositing them before the throne, there were 120 talents of gold, large quantities of exotic spices never seen in Israel before, and chests of precious stones.

The king bowed to her in acknowledgment, and she bowed to him in deference. Her attendants then escorted her back to her suite to change for the arduous journey home.

He hoped they would meet again someday.

After Her Departure

That night, his dreams were filled with images of black and white striped ponies and dusky maidens with fiery black eyes. He awoke more tired than rested.

As he struggled to get out of bed, he muttered to himself, "Back to reality. There's much work to catch up on now that she has gone." But he wasn't excited about it.

After stumbling to his nightstand, Solomon studied himself in the mirror that hung on the wall above it. Something silvery in his hair caught his eye.

"What's this?" He isolated it from the surrounding strands of jet-black hair.

"I'm becoming an old man!" he exclaimed with shock and then declared resolutely, "This cannot happen! I have not even begun to live..." at which his voice trailed off into a hopeless sigh.

Fatherhood

Meanwhile, all the children he had sired by his many wives and mistresses were growing up. He established schools in which the boys were instructed in law, commerce, the arts, and science. He saw that the girls learned to read and write, and he allowed them to pursue whatever interested them—as long as they first mastered domestic arts such as stitching and caring for younger siblings. The most beautiful were given in marriage to foreign rulers in treaty exchanges. When their father's reign was over, those unmarried would be on their own.

Of all his sons, Rehoboam received his favor—if not his undivided attention. The firstborn of Queen Adona, Solomon expected him to reign as the next king of Israel. Through him, the promise must come.

But he was an immature boy who sorely tested the king's patience. While well-educated and handsome, he often lacked common sense.

"How can you teach a child good judgment, Simeon?" he asked his friend in exasperation as they had another one of their walks in the palace gardens.

Thoughtfully, Simeon replied, "Maybe your Rehoboam will learn it only through making mistakes. That is, you know, how most of us learn!" he smiled and gave a sideways look at Solomon. The king, in all his God-given wisdom, couldn't comprehend that. He still viewed the Gift as somehow enabling him to bypass such unpleasant methods of acquiring wisdom.

Resolution

That night, unsettling thoughts of his son's weaknesses aside, Solomon lit his lamp and pulled out of his desk drawer the story of his Lady of Shunam—The Song of Songs. He didn't want to keep it in the palace anymore. Its proximity—in contrast to the great distance between him and Deborah—gnawed at him and left him restless beyond his ability to bear it.

"I will bury it far away from here," he concluded. Searching his mind for a proper repository, the image of Moshe and his family, in the little village of Kephirah, came before him. "There must be many caves in the mountains near the village in which it can be hidden. I'll take it there...and use the opportunity to renew old acquaintances." The decision having been made, he extinguished the lamp and sought the comfort of his bed. He would sleep alone tonight.

In the Darkness

Do you think you can so easily escape your pain? Traeh screamed soundlessly into Solomon's soul, his hatred for the king growing daily. *Think again, you fool!* As Traeh's claws dug deeper into his heart, the hounded king moaned in his sleep.

CHAPTER SIXTEEN

KEPHIRAH AGAIN

I n spite of the fear that mysteriously clung to his heart, Solomon would indeed return to Kephirah—this time in a grand chariot pulled by three pairs of sleek Arabian stallions. Even though the last few miles would have to be made over the dusty, rutted road that took up where his paved road ended, he would press on in royal style, determined to play the role to the hilt. This time, Moshe would be duly impressed with the "king in disguise" whom he had entertained nearly twenty years before.

The countryside was breathtakingly beautiful at this time of the year. Springtime always brought blooms to the cactus and patchy meadows of lush green grass, which the shepherds quickly pursued with hungry flocks close on their heels. The air was clear and still somewhat cool, carrying the scent of the yellow flowers that popped up along the roadway and waved in the breeze without a care in the world.

A Roadside Lesson

It was also the time of year when farmers tilled the land and planted seeds for the crops they hoped to harvest in the fall. Teams of oxen broke up the ground that had lain fallow over the winter. The smell of freshly turned sod quickened the pulse of every man who knew the secret of seedtime and harvest—that his work would be rewarded with bounty for his family's table and would bring him esteem among his neighbors. He knew that it all began with diligence in the moment of opportunity when the soil was just right for tilling and before the spring rains.

Soon after Solomon's entourage left Jerusalem behind, the king became absorbed in assessing the condition of the land to his left and right. He knew well the strength, and even power, that resided in the nation that could provide for itself agriculturally. As they passed by field after field, he waved encouragingly at the tillers and sowers as they labored diligently in preparing the waiting earth. He was pleased by what he saw.

"Wise men, these," he commented with obvious satisfaction to Nathaniel, the servant sitting to his left in the chariot.

"Yes, Your Majesty," was the boy's prompt reply.

But as they passed the boundary marker of one of the farms where all were hard at work, they came upon the land belonging to Jonah Haddasha. A frown overtook the king's countenance, and it soon turned to disgust. The condition of *this* man's land was appalling.

"Eli!" he shouted to his driver from his cushioned seat behind the man with the reins. "Pull over to the side of the road at once!"

Eli immediately reined in the prancing steeds and eased the chariot off the pavement and onto the grassy ridge along the road. Solomon—his robes drawn up and gathered in his left hand as he steadied himself with his right—carefully climbed down from the chariot. He then strode over to the broken-down stone fence and eyed it with disgust. Obviously annoyed, he scanned the field in front of him that was overgrown with weeds, no more than a home for jackals.

He knew the man who owned this field. He had known Jonah since childhood when, even as now, the fellow could never seem to attend to anything he possessed. He had been notorious for losing his scrolls and for failing to study his lessons. More than once, Simeon had told Solomon stories about how Jonah was disciplined by the rabbi for neglecting to memorize the assigned portions of the law which governed their people. Jonah had preferred to dream his days away regardless of the penalty. The boy—and the man he had become—had no ambition.

"See this, my friend?" he spoke sternly to Nathaniel, who stood at his side ready to do his bidding. "This man is lazy and foolish! He sleeps or twiddles his thumbs while others plant and till. Come fall, he'll cry for handouts from everyone else because he will have no harvest of his own." The king spat in disgust into the sand at his feet. Then cocking his head to look fully into the young man's face, he warned, "Remember this lesson: He who works his land will have abundant food, but he who chases fantasies lacks judgment. The sluggard craves and gets nothing, but the desires of the diligent are fully satisfied."

Nathaniel began to sweat under the king's vehemence and he immediately determined never to be like the owner of this land and incur the wrath of the king!

"Mark my words," Solomon finally concluded, "diligent hands will rule, but laziness ends in slave labor! If this negligence were rampant in Israel, we'd soon all be slaves to some nation with more sense!" he added gravely, more to himself this time than to Nathaniel. Turning on his heels, the king headed back to the chariot, with Nathaniel hustling to keep up in order to show that he was certainly no Jonah Haddasha.

Welcomed Peace

The country, for the most part, had a calming effect on the king, who sometimes had a difficult time relaxing and simply enjoying his accomplishments. This day, however, he put all thoughts of kingdom-building and foreign enterprise aside and simply drank in the serenity of the distant hills and the green valley that lay ahead of him as he traveled on to Kephirah.

Just outside the village, Eli slowed the horses to a walk before proceeding sedately into the center of town and up to the village well. As memories flooded Solomon's thoughts, he disembarked and smiled reassuringly at the gawking villagers, who thought they had never had a visit from so grand a guest before.

A smile flashed across Solomon's face as he remembered how mothers had protectively corralled their daughters to keep them away from him the last time he had visited this village. This time, women—young and old—pressed in to catch a glimpse of him in a simple, but fine, embroidered tunic with a scarlet robe draped casually across his shoulders. For the most part, the men and boys preferred to investigate every aspect of the golden chariot and stare in amazement at the fine horses. All in all, the king enjoyed the attention, as did Eli and Nathaniel, whose chests were puffed out with pride at being part of the royal company.

Solomon's eyes anxiously ranged over the crowd, searching for Moshe or Miriam. Just as he was about to conclude that they were not to be found, he spied them standing on the outer rim of the crowd. Their graying hair reminded Solomon of the passage of time since they had met and parted. But regardless of whatever changes in appearance aging could effect, he would have known them anywhere.

"Moshe! Miriam!" he shouted with delight. "Come here!" At that, the crowd split and the stunned pair slowly made their way to the waiting monarch. Neither of them, however, showed any sign of recognition, other than that this must surely be the legendary King Solomon in person.

"Don't you remember me?" he asked with obvious disappointment. They responded with red faces and an attempt at an apology, totally baffled that the king should be so personal with them.

"I visited in your home many years ago, dressed as a shepherd on his way to the Hills of Ephraim." Still seeing no recognition in their eyes, he grabbed Moshe's hand and looked him hard in the eye. "Remember the proverbs I wrote on parchment and left with a gold coin on your table before slipping out into the night after you had gone to bed?"

Suddenly Moshe's face lit up. "It was *you*?" he asked incredulously, instinctively withdrawing his hand in embarrassment and awe. "You, the King of Israel, ate at my table and listened for hours to my silly ramblings?"

"But they *weren't* silly ramblings, Moshe!" the king insisted with sincerity. "You gave me one of the most interesting conversations I have ever enjoyed! I loved your stories of the village and I deeply valued your love of chronicling them." Taking Moshe's hand again, Solomon held it fast. "How goes the writing, Carpenter? Are the piles of parchments reaching the rafters yet?" he asked fondly. "Isn't writing a wonderful gift?"

Oblivious to the crowd, Moshe began to relax as he embraced this voice and face as he had at their first meeting. Joyfully, they exchanged highlights of all that had happened during the past twenty years. After a nudge from

Miriam that reminded him of his manners, he apologized and quickly issued an invitation. "You must come to our home for dinner. Will you again grace our table?" Then breaking into a big grin, he added, "My wife can *still* make out of nothing a feast fit for a king!"

All three of them burst out laughing, as they remembered how Moshe had so naively spoken this classic line the other time he had unwittingly invited the king to dinner!

"I was just waiting for you to ask!" the king replied with a sweeping bow to the carpenter and his wife that brought a cheer from the crowd.

As for Solomon, he had never felt more alive than he did that day—save when he had discovered his true love in the vineyards above another simple village not far from this one. But for this moment, he was simply delighted to be with his old friends. For this moment, he could almost forget his sorrow and the weight of being king.

Together Again

And so he dined with them on a meal that was indeed fit for a king. Miriam really outdid herself—with the help of her now-grown daughters who either still lived at home or were married to a villager and lived nearby. They pooled their resources and dined on freshly roasted lamb with all the trimmings, topped off with mounds of succulent pomegranates, grapes, and figs, and accented with the sweetest wine Solomon had ever tasted.

After the wonderful meal, everyone, especially Moshe's sons, got into the act of entertaining the king. One of the boys, Zebulon, was a juggler of no mean talent. Up into the air flew everything from his mother's clay dishes to his father's tools, with several kept in the air at once by this dexterous lad. Never did he drop a single one! The rest of the family set a lively cadence for him by chanting and clapping their hands in rhythm.

Laughter rang through the simple cottage and stories abounded. Solomon couldn't remember when he'd had such a delightful time since his father, David, had entertained his mighty men in the old palace. Their tales of valor and the intrigues of the desert campaigns had fascinated the young boy. He had hoped to grow up to be like them. But he was always different, inescapably different, it seemed. His was another era requiring another mindset and different talents. But forever, he wished he could have been more like them.

As the evening drew to a close, Solomon approached his reason for coming again. He pushed back his chair, let Miriam fill his glass with the delicious wine one more time, and began.

"Moshe, I come with a request of you that I hope you won't consider foolish." The room grew quiet. The rest of the family retired to the one other room in the house so the two men could talk privately. Moshe and the king sat adjacent to each other at the head of the worn dinner table.

"I want you to help me bury something," he stated simply. Seeing the quizzical look on his host's face, he added, "It's a manuscript...a love story that I have written about an encounter that seems now to have occurred a million years ago." He leaned toward Moshe and spoke in barely audible tones that Moshe had to strain to hear. "The story haunts me." The king rubbed his temples with his fingertips and then reached across the corner of the table and put his hand on Moshe's arm. "I can't keep it with me anymore, yet I can't bring myself to destroy it," he continued in an intense whisper. Moshe knew only to wait and listen.

"Will you bury it for me in a safe place, or hide it in a cave where no one will find it?" Drawing back his hand and rubbing his temples again, he added, "There must be someplace like that around here. And you are the only one I know to ask to do this very important favor." The king, now saddened by his memories, paused to let Moshe think it over. Then he asked, "Do you know of such a place?"

Mission Accomplished

And so it was that the beautiful, poignant *Song of Songs* found a resting place in a cave deep in the gentle mountains between Kephirah and Gibeon. There the manuscript remained for hundreds of years—secured with a simple seal that Moshe applied to the yellowing scroll and wrapped tightly in a soft, waterproof lambskin.

Solomon, Eli, and Nathaniel returned to Jerusalem, with barely a word passing among them. The king was, in spirit, somewhere off wending his way through lush vineyards on the distant hills above a little town called Shunam. He was saying good-bye to a dream, and it was breaking his heart.

Of Things to Come

It was three o'clock in the afternoon when his chariot reached the outskirts of Jerusalem. The ritual of preparing for the evening sacrifice at the Dwelling was underway. He had been taught as a child at his parents' knees that a life must be given to atone for sins that, when committed, made communion with Jehovah impossible. Sinful man could not stand in the presence of a holy God.

But because Jehovah loved them, his father had told him, He had made provision for a substitute so that no man or woman, boy or girl, would have to die for his or her sins.

A simple, pure lamb without defect—representing a worthy sacrifice—was to be given to the priest by each family in exchange for the forgiveness of their sins that day. The priest then laid his hands on the lamb's head as a symbol of passing the sins of the family onto the lamb who would die in their place. For centuries, this had been Israel's practice.

As the king neared the city and heard the bleating of the sheep about to be slain, he remembered something else his father had often said as the hour of sacrifice drew near.

"Someday, Messiah will come!" King David had said with excitement. "He will be perfect, just as the lamb, and He will die for our sins once and for all! Only Messiah, God's own Son, has the ability to end this wretched cycle of sin and death. He will break the power of evil in our lives with His love and set us free!"

Memories of the vision that had played out in the night sky nearly forty years before—of the Shepherd on the crossed beams and the King and the Lamb upon the golden throne—flooded his heart.

Help me understand that vision, Promise Giver, the sad king begged as his chariot passed through the gates of the mystical city. *Help me, please!*

Immediately, he felt an infinite, unseen arm of love drawing him close. ***Someday, when you have faced the demons within and refused them the right to make you suffer, you will understand. When your own way is spent, the pain will end.***

The king's back stiffened at the thought that he couldn't find his own way out of the pain. He shook off the Presence and quickly sought his chambers.

"Human arms, that's what I need right now!" he declared to his personal servant. "Bring me a woman from my harem," he ordered.

The servant looked questioningly at the king, hesitant to act without more specific instructions.

"Any one will do!" he barked back.

———————————

Traeh emitted a hideous gasp of relief as Solomon once again refused to surrender to Promise Giver and be healed. "This hell would be complete with such a fool beside me," he wheezed disgustedly as he kicked out of his way one of the myriad of annoying, groveling, and disfigured demons that forever hung in his shadow.

Chapter Seventeen

Rumblings of Discontent

The years ground relentlessly on. The single strand of silver hair Solomon had discovered long ago had multiplied until his raven mane glistened with the silver tones that had come to dominate.

To compensate for the life he was losing, and in an attempt to silence the warning voice of Jehovah, the king seized every moment as if it were his last. Wine, women, and song drove his nights, and the amassing of wealth, naively at others' expense, consumed his days. The favored lived in opulence and thought little of it, while the poor struggled to exist.

His conscience seemed to be asleep.

An Appeal

Council meetings with his advisors became increasingly labored.

"My liege," the now-ancient and ailing Micah ventured one particularly cold morning in the winter of the king's thirtieth year of reign. "Don't you think that the taxes you have levied against your own people—not to mention those against the aliens within our borders—have become exorbitant?" His voice crackled with age. He looked anxiously about the table hoping someone else would chime in and back him up. But none did. Only the youngest among them, Jeroboam, looked to be at all sympathetic to his appeal. For good or ill, the assertive young man was creating his own following of the disaffected. Micah had fully expected Jeroboam to support his protest this day. But, at least for the moment, it appeared that he was in it alone.

At the other end of the table, the king leaned heavily forward upon his elbows and stared dully back at Micah. Each breath he drew resonated, heard by all in the room. The excessive weight his once-slender frame now carried caused his breathing to come with effort, especially when he felt challenged or annoyed. This time, he was simply annoyed.

"Have I not treated you well, old man?" he asked with a hint of steel in his otherwise passionless voice. "Has not your every need been met and is not your family secure in comfort?" His stare persisted without interruption. Micah flinched as the stare clung to his heart.

"Of course, my king, of course!" he nervously agreed. "But our nation is becoming economically polarized, and I fear an uprising if you do not lessen the burden upon those who labor to sustain the kingdom." There, he had said it and he wasn't sorry.

But the king simply continued to stare back at him.

Finally, Solomon sighed and turned his eyes to the window through which gray daylight could be seen, while the sound of wind whistled about the eaves of the palace. With a wave of his hand in Micah's direction, the king simply dismissed the appeal.

Suddenly, Jeroboam rose to his feet—a bit uncertainly at first, but gaining confidence as he gathered his thoughts and prepared to speak in opposition to the king who had brought him on as a promising future leader. In the few short years he had been an understudy to the seasoned men on the council, he had seen the seamy side of the venerated King Solomon. His own ambition had made the most of it.

"I agree with Micah, Your Majesty," he began. "This cannot continue without grave consequences!"

"Sit down, you upstart!" shouted the king, suddenly incensed by the defiance of the young man. "Do you think I don't know that you use your relationship with me to gain influence with those who oppose me? You're just lucky I allow you on the council at all," he seethed.

"Then I don't want to be on your ridiculous council anymore," Jeroboam continued steadily in response to Solomon's insinuation. "Do what you want, as you always do, but I will no longer be a party to your selfishness!" Every other council member sat speechlessly by this astounding exchange between the king and his young protégé.

"Then get out!" Solomon thundered as he slammed his beefy fist down on the gold-covered table.

"With pleasure!" Jeroboam shot back as he resolutely turned from the table and strode out the door.

"See to it that all his property is seized at once and his followers threatened or jailed," he quickly instructed Daniel, his Director of Land and Property. And to the rest, he bellowed, "Make his life impossible! He must not enjoy another peaceful moment in this country I have built!"

The Fugitive

And so it was that Jeroboam, the ambitious young man of great promise—who had risen from Curator of the Walls to Overseer of the Tribe of Joseph and member of the king's council—chose exile in Egypt in preference to being tormented in his native land. Sadly, the fugitive resigned himself to a life apart from all those he had ever known and loved. Perhaps he was not destined for greatness in his own country as he had supposed.

A Few Years Later

After Jeroboam had settled into life in his new country, he had a strange dream. He dreamed that a massive purple cloth, one so large it covered the deserts and valleys of Israel, was stretched taut from border to border of the Kingdom of Israel. He was himself suspended above the scene, weightless, supported by nothing truly visible.

In the next moment, two hands, as of a giant beyond earthly proportions, reached down, took hold of the cloth and tore it into twelve pieces! As Jeroboam waited in suspense to understand this wonder, one of the hands stretched forth to where he was suspended in space and thrust ten of the pieces into his arms!

He awoke at dawn in a sweat, excited yet fearful. And then the memory of an event of his youth—completely disregarded since his exile—came back to him in vivid detail. He arose, bathed and dressed hurriedly, and rushed out to his favorite grove where he often went to reflect. No one would be there at this hour.

This was the memory: Years ago, an odd old prophet by the name of Ahijah from Shilo had accosted him with a salute as he had passed through the gates of Jerusalem. Following their brief greeting, Ahijah had taken him to a place out of the way of travelers, where there was no one who could overhear or watch them. The prophet proceeded to take off his robe—a beautiful and obviously newly woven garment. As Jeroboam had watched in curiosity, the gray-bearded and stooped prophet had torn the elegant purple robe into twelve pieces and told him, "This is the will of God; He will part the dominion of Solomon and give one

160

tribe, with that which is next to it, to Solomon's son because of the promise made to David for his succession. This will be so that David may always have a lamp before him in Jerusalem, the city where he chose to place his name. However, He will give ten tribes to you, Jeroboam, because Solomon has sinned against Him and given himself up to foreign women and their gods."

Jeroboam recalled being stunned and somewhat amused by the whole conversation. The king had been, at that time, leading Israel with spiritual fervor and devotion to Jehovah. His transgressions were no more than were common even among the godly. Everyone was in love with him and calling him a god because of the insight and wisdom he exhibited in ruling his people. *Who could have foreseen the days that eventually came upon us?* he mused as he sat in the cool shadow of a dense cluster of palm trees, which gave shelter to the image of one of the many expressionless stone gods that inhabited every grove and courtyard in Egypt.

And what else had the prophet said? Ah, yes. "As long as you do whatever God commands you and walk in His ways and do what is right, He will be with you. He will build you a dynasty as enduring as the one He built for David and give Israel to you. He will humble David's descendants because of this, but not forever." Jeroboam smiled as he remembered that last line: "He will humble David's descendants..."

And finally, "Be righteous and keep the laws, because Jehovah has proposed to you the greatest of all rewards for your trust in Him. And the honor you must pay to God, exalting Him as you know David did."

Suddenly, he felt very foolish keeping company with the god of stone a few feet away from the bench upon which he sat. He hastily rose and returned to his quarters. From this day forward, he would prepare for the death of the king so that he could claim the prophet's word. The timing of his return to Israel would have to be carefully choreographed so as to influence the greatest number of the disaffected of his countrymen.

But will they remember me when I return? he worried. He would have to take that risk and trust the prophet's word.

Back in Jerusalem

Meanwhile, Solomon brooded, but would not repent. He stubbornly persisted in believing that his vast contributions to Jewish and world culture in the areas of literature, trade, government, science, and horticulture were more than enough to validate his every decision. *After all*, he often told himself when doubts dared to creep into his heart, *Jehovah gave me the Gift.*

With this fact, no one could argue. But behind closed doors, many in his kingdom wondered at his use of it. The eldest remembered the conditions that had accompanied the Gift, even though Solomon seemed to have forgotten—that if the king did not follow Jehovah with his whole heart and walk in the ways of his father, David, the kingdom would be torn from his hands and divided. Many who had heard David himself speak of this before the people, trembled at the thought of the harvest that would come from the king's flagrantly sowing seeds of disregard for Jehovah, which increased as he grew older.

While Solomon and his friends were consumed with material profit, Traeh rejoiced as he spent his days speaking lies into the old king's heart.

Jehovah didn't mean what He said back then, Traeh hissed slowly, driving every word into Solomon's heart with precision. *Didn't He say that He would forever love you and be a father to you?*

Knowing that he had the king's ear for every word, he pressed his advantage and went for the old man's ego. *What would He do without you? Haven't you caused men of every nation to fear His name? Why, you have made Him proud of you by your amazing use of the Gift!*

As the susceptible heart of the king embraced every word, deeming his triumphs far above his shortcomings, all the demons in hell cheered raucously. They sparred with one another in mock warfare, each determined to best the other in stealing the king's heart entirely.

And the king slid closer to the abyss.

CHAPTER EIGHTEEN

THE DARK PIT OF DESPAIR

Not long after Jeroboam's departure, the king summoned his old friend again. Simeon found Solomon alone in the palace gardens, back in the area where he had first heard the haunting screech of the king's enigmatic peacocks. Since then, many other exotic birds had been added to the collection. At times, the cacophony of the feathered menagerie was thoroughly disconcerting to the quiet and gentle Simeon.

How can he think in such a distracting place? Simeon asked himself as he followed the winding pathway toward the bench on which the king sat, his head in his hands, eyes fixed on the ground at his feet.

"Solomon, how are you?" he inquired as he seated himself on another bench opposite the monarch.

Solomon's hair, completely silver now, was uncombed. Indeed, his entire appearance was unkempt, from his wrinkled tunic, which hung limply over his heavy frame, to his unwashed feet.

When the king didn't respond, Simeon tried another approach. "I see you have added to your collection of rare birds," he began, searching for a way to engage the despondent figure before him. "Which is your favorite?"

Slowly, the king lifted his head as his arms dropped heavily to his side, and his hands came to rest in his lap. He didn't look directly at Simeon, nor did it appear that he was looking at anything in particular...just staring into space without seeing.

If the eyes are the windows of the soul, thought Simeon, *it is as though the lights have gone out within this once-mighty man.*

A great sigh welled up from the depths of the old monarch's emptiness and slipped slowly through his half-parted lips.

In a voice as lifeless and as dark as his eyes, he muttered, "I wish I were dead, Simeon."

Simeon, shocked into silence, simply listened and waited. He didn't know what to say.

Solomon continued, his breathing becoming more noticeably labored. "You're my only friend, Simeon," he said with a sad smile for his friend. "I've lived a long and ambitious life, haven't I?" The smile began to fade. "I've traveled the world over, entertained dignitaries from every nation, commissioned thousands of officers, and gone to bed with more women than I can count, and yet I have only one friend!"

The king returned to rubbing his temples with his fingertips as though to ease some terrible pain. "My sons will live and die, and their sons after them, and who will remember us when you are gone?" Then turning to Simeon with a tormented look, he issued the ultimate question:

"What has been the use of it all?"

Still, Simeon sat silently, thus far unable to enter this desperate conversation.

After a long pause during which the king searched his old friend's eyes, he begged, "Tell me, please, why do I have this awful hole in my heart?" He shook his head slowly as he pursued his dismal reflections, hunting for the root of his sorrow. Simeon listened, searching his own heart for a response, should he be asked for one or be given an opportunity to speak his own concerns about the state of the dear man before him whom he had loved for a lifetime.

The king, not yet ready for any response from Simeon, continued, "I used to think it was caused by the loss of Deborah, but that fantasy is at rest in a cave in the mountains above Kephirah. I thought my vow to never love again caused it as well...so, in time, I *tried* to abandon the vow and give my heart to a thousand others—but still the pit deepened."

Energized by the thoughts that came next, Solomon delved into another paradox. "Haven't I done wonderful things for Israel? Haven't all my childhood dreams come true?

"Hasn't my wisdom astounded the nations?" he continued, pleading for affirmation. "Hasn't it fattened our coffers with gold and brought us the finery of the world? Isn't that what Jehovah wanted?" But then his voice dropped to a whisper and tears welled up in his eyes as he said simply, "Yet the gold no longer glitters, does it, my old friend? The mines could become barren and I wouldn't care."

He surprised Simeon then by rising suddenly and laughing as though at a great joke. Simeon rose instinctively in response, not knowing what to expect next.

"With all my discoveries, I have found nothing that God did not know about before I was ever on the face of the earth! Every new thing I thought *I* discovered was old before I found it and will be forgotten in time, merely to be discovered again by some fool who, like me, thinks he is very clever!

"And do you know what?" he asked rhetorically, again not expecting an answer but rather answering it himself.

"It's absolutely useless to make life turn out right...the way you want it to be. I tried to create a perfect world for imperfect men, but their imperfections...my imperfections...continually polluted every endeavor."

He dropped his head, his silver-bearded chin resting on his chest for a moment. Then, drawing a deep breath and letting it out in a puff, he stated simply to his friend, "I am no creator, Simeon, no creator at all. What is twisted in the hearts of men cannot be straightened by me; what is lacking cannot be counted if it doesn't exist."

They began walking slowly toward the garden entrance that opened back into the palace. As they made their way, side by side, the king drifted back into philosophizing.

"You see," he tried to explain, "I thought the Gift absolved me from error—that I alone of all mortals could pursue anything I desired in the name of knowledge and remain untouched by its evil!" At that, he laughed loudly in self-derision. "What an incredible fool I have been!"

Abruptly, the king dismissed Simeon with one last word. "We will talk more about this at another time, my dear friend. Today, I fear what you might say to me about these matters. I may, in time, be able to bear your insights. Please be patient with me."

So Simeon left with having given no more than a greeting and a question about peacocks, a question so irrelevant that the king had not deigned to answer it. He tried not to feel that he had failed his friend.

At His Desk Again

That evening, instead of pursuing futile entertainment with the opportunists who surrounded him in the city of David, Solomon continued his dismal ruminations on parchment. He began at night where his daytime conversation had ended.

Meaningless! Meaningless! His quill pen scratched out the words on the fresh scroll that he spread out before him on the treasured writing desk he had inherited from his father.

Utterly meaningless! Everything is meaningless, he wrote. Huge tears welled up in his eyes as the thought of all his seemingly wasted effort to use the Gift diligently.

What does man gain from all his labor at which he toils under the sun? he continued, struggling to see his own handwriting through the tears.

> *Generations come and generations go, but the earth remains forever. The sun rises and the sun sets, and hurries back to where it rises. The wind blows to the south and turns to the north; round and round it goes, ever returning on its course. All streams flow into the sea, yet the sea is never full. To the place the streams come from, there they return again. All things are wearisome, more than one can say.*[24]

His head drooped from the very weariness of the words, and his eyes burned from fatigue. Lacking the energy to undress for bed, he simply laid his heavy head on the crook of his arm and fell asleep slumped over his desk. The ink well was left uncovered, and the script upon the parchment remained unblotted, as the desperate monarch—child of David and child of Jehovah—slept and dreamed of a simple shepherd and cross-beams in a starless sky.

---

24.   Ecclesiastes 1:4-8.

In the Morning

The king was awakened by a servant gently urging him to bathe and dress. He had no idea what time it was. Just then, his attention was caught by the pungent aroma of a tray of goat cheese, coconut milk, and figs the servant had placed on a table near the open window, and he realized he was hungry. He awkwardly got to his feet, discovering that his back and legs were sore and stiff from the night spent at his desk. However, Solomon managed to walk over to the table where his breakfast was waiting.

Deciding to eat the cheese and figs while lying down on his bed rather than sitting again as he had all night, he carried the tray to his bedside stand. As he stretched out on the wondrously comforting feather bed and ran his hands appreciatively over the silk sheets, he noticed that his ankles were swollen.

The servant noticed as well. "The swelling will go down if you will just rest a bit," he assured the king. "Just lift your feet for me while I put pillows under them, elevating them so the swelling will go down faster."

The disheveled king obliged without question. After the servant laid out a fresh tunic and robe, Solomon dismissed him with a promise that he would bathe as soon as he felt rested.

While he lay there, with a slender slice of cheese in one hand and a fig in the other, his usually ever-present appetite suddenly left him. He turned onto his side and stretched to put the food back on the tray.

Suddenly, as in days of old, the mystic sound of his father's voice wafted through the room and seeped into his soul. How he missed his father!

"I would give every horse, every chariot, every piece of gold and every gem in the kingdom to be a child at his knee once again," he whispered wistfully.

Praise the Lord, O my soul, and forget not all His benefits—
who forgives all your sins
and heals all your diseases,
who redeems your life from the pit
and crowns you with love and compassion,
who satisfies your desires with good things
so that your youth is renewed like the eagle's.[25]

But as the song unfolded and caressed his aching heart, the oft-forgotten amulet that had hung from his neck for some thirty years burned into his soul. Some strange force within it fought against the song with frightening strength, causing the words to become disjointed and indistinguishable! His mind became confused.

The old king's heart felt pain—which he dismissed as severe heartburn from the overly rich meals he had been eating of late. He struggled in vain to hear the rest of the song as his attention was consumed with trying to prop himself up into a sitting position to ease the agonizing sensation in his chest.

As soon as the song ceased, the pain ceased as well. Solomon breathed a sigh of relief and wiped the tears from his eyes with his rumpled shirtsleeve. He then fell asleep.

As the Attack Continues

Somewhere, in the depths of slumber, the monarch dreamed a hideous dream—of demonic dragons dancing on the roof of the Dwelling. He awoke with a start, drenched

---

25. Psalm 103:2-5.

171

in sweat, fear in his soul, the amulet stuck to the skin over his heart. With enormous resolve he arose, bathed, and dressed.

"I will not lose my mind," he fairly shouted. "I refuse to succumb to insanity while there is breath left in this body!" As he shed his tunic and stumbled toward his bathing pool, he muttered, "Somehow I will make sense of this. Somehow I will find peace."

As he slipped into the tepid water and felt its soothing effects, a thought came to him. "I'll talk to someone about this...someone at a distance enough to see it all objectively."

After quickly bathing and donning clean clothes, he called for his courier. Hastily, he penned a note to the Queen of Sheba.

> *May I pay a personal visit to you—all internation-*
> *al business aside? This time, I seek your insights.*
> *King Solomon*

He affixed his seal and handed it to the courier who was soon at his door.

Solomon was so certain she would welcome his visit, he set about making plans for the long trip even before receiving her reply.

Her response came in little more than a fortnight.

> *King Solomon,*
>
> *Please come. It will be a pleasure to converse with*
> *you again. I cannot say that I will have any insight*
> *of value for you, but I will thoroughly enjoy our dis-*
> *cussions. I will be in residence for the next three*
> *months. Come at your convenience.*
>
> *Queen of Sheba*

One week after receiving her reply, Solomon was ready to travel. His party would include guards, provisions, and a great store of gifts for the queen. They would go by camel caravan to the sea, and then by ship to Ethiopia. There they would then enlist another caravan to travel inland. The adventure alone would raise his spirits, he was sure.

CHAPTER NINETEEN

A REVEALING ADVENTURE

The sea air was so refreshing. "This is wonderful!" the king exclaimed to his companion at the rail of the great sailing ship. Then to himself, he whispered, "To be away from everything manmade—to gaze upon the vast and unspoiled waters—inspires me to embrace life again."

But on the second day at sea, Solomon began feeling uneasy. A strange foreboding grew steadily in his soul. *What is it?* he anxiously asked himself as he searched the sky overhead, shading his eyes from the blazing sun. Slowly it came to him. *Something is amiss back in Israel.* The impression was unmistakably clear. His old heart pounded with apprehension.

He sought out the captain up on the forward deck. The weathered Phoenician seaman bowed respectfully to the king while continuing to keep his eyes on the horizon.

"It's been a fine trip, Captain Monehan. You have lived up to your reputation as an astute leader of your crew and as a skilled navigator," the king began. He preferred that the captain be in a good mood to handle the order he was about to give.

The captain beamed with pride and bowed again. "It has been my pleasure to serve you," he responded with a toothy smile.

Solomon drew a deep breath and forged on. "But, we must turn back." Before the captain could ask any questions he couldn't answer, Solomon tried to explain.

"You are a man of instincts, Captain, as am I." He paused briefly, trying to find the words to explain the alteration in plans to the one other man who had invested a great deal in making this voyage. "I sense that something dire is transpiring in Israel in my absence and I must return as soon as possible."

"I see, Sir," the gruff seaman responded, remembering the time when he too had changed course on a premonition— an action that had spared him great losses when an unexpected storm struck the sea where they would have been sailing. "I will do as you say," he added obligingly, respecting the monarch all the more for being true to his instincts.

Immediately, this man of few words set about plotting the best route of return, considering the winds and the time of year. The ship was soon turned about and on its way back home.

Somewhere in the Desert

Jeroboam had heard the news in Egypt that the king would be out of the country for several months.

"Now is the time to make our move," he told the dozen or so fellow exiles who had joined themselves to his cause in their own attempt at revenge on the King of Israel who had turned them out of the country for their petty crimes and whose judicial system had ostracized them.

Ever since the prophetic dream had returned, Jeroboam had been corresponding with the disaffected back home, keeping them stirred up and anxious to revolt. He estimated their number at over 10,000 men ready to follow him in battle.

As his supporters in Egypt and Israel traveled to meet one another in Sinai, spirits were high.

"There they are!" Bartar shouted when he spied the caravan from Israel in the distance across the shimmering sand. They were but a speck on the horizon, but Bartar could not be dissuaded as to their identity.

And he was not disappointed. They were indeed a contingency of their exiled leader's supporters coming to escort them all the way to Jerusalem.

What They Didn't Know

But Solomon had already reached land and Israel's western border. He was in the process of preparing his own caravan for the trip back to Jerusalem. He was well ahead of Jeroboam and his men.

When Jeroboam was still two days out from the city, a messenger sent by his sympathizers in Jerusalem found the campsite where he and his contingency had decided to rest and finalize their plans for taking over the city.

"You are all in big trouble!" the young courier shouted as he hastily dismounted his donkey and tossed the reins to one of the animal handlers at the camp. Jeroboam, hearing the shouting, ran toward the stranger to see what was wrong.

"He's on his way back!" the courier continued breathlessly.

"*Who's* on his way back? What are you talking about?" Jeroboam interrogated the young man, grabbing him by the shoulders to calm him down.

"King Solomon!" he answered quickly. "He'll be in Jerusalem before you are!"

Fear stole into Jeroboam's eyes as he began to grasp the implications. After a few quick decisions, he turned to his men and immediately issued orders. "Hurry and eat, then pack up. Those of you from Israel, go on to your homes before any more questions are raised about your absence."

Then, singling out those who had accompanied him from Egypt, he outlined a plan for their own survival. "The rest of us will head for the caves that pockmark the ragged hills south of Beersheba. We'll hide out there," he reassured them, "until it's safe to travel again."

Putting his hand on the shoulder of the tired courier, Jeroboam urged him to eat something and then take a short nap before returning to Jerusalem. "Tell Heman, your master, to send food to us in the caves while we regroup." When the boy looked at him questioningly, he replied, "Don't worry. He will know the place where we will be hiding." Jeroboam's mind flashed back to the time he had first been sent out of Israel. Heman had gone with him as far as the caves and had sent him on his way well supplied. He was a true friend.

Disappointed and a bit disgruntled that their plan wasn't working, but confident in Jeroboam's leadership, they all obeyed without an argument.

Sometime Later

Jeroboam and his men waited in the caves until they were sure that Solomon did not know of their whereabouts and would not be pursuing them. They carefully made their way—traveling only at night, back to Egypt. They would wait there for the king's death.

Their one consolation was that the number of supporters was growing steadily in Israel. Next time, they'd return in power, received openly and with joy by the people.

Back in Jerusalem

Solomon burst into the council meeting with fire in his eyes.

"What's going on?" he probed one face after another. Each looked back at him as though they knew nothing.

Silas, the newest member of the council, spoke first. "Your Majesty, what do you mean?" he asked innocently. "Nothing has changed since you left! We are merely doing business as usual," he said coolly.

Barak shot him a sideways glance but said nothing.

The king exploded, "Something's amiss and I demand to know what it is!"

Again, it was Silas who answered for them all. "I fear that your imagination has gotten the best of you," he replied with an attempt at a respectfully comforting tone. "Truly, all is well," he lied.

Solomon turned on his heel and left the room. He promptly order the guards doubled at all entrances to the city and put on high alert around the country, especially along Israel's rambling borders.

Only after his orders had been carried out could he rest. He decided not to attempt another trip to Ethiopia; he needed to stay at home and protect his throne.

Privately

Nightly, before the lamp was snuffed out and regardless of which wife he would be sleeping with, the king was haunted by the fact that life was not turning out as he had planned. His son, Rehoboam, was weak-willed and immature, and certainly not ready to rule in his stead if something happened to him.

As he lingered at his window, peering into the darkness over the city of David—the jewel of Israel—it dawned on the disillusioned king that he was helpless to alter the course of the nation's future. He could not undo the choices he had made. The rules Jehovah had laid down for kings long before he was born—rules he had learned as a child, but then promptly forgotten as an adult—rose to condemn him when he tried to sleep.

That night, for the first time in thirty years, Solomon pulled from his closet a scroll that he had written himself when he was first crowned king. For the first five years of his reign, he had obediently read it aloud each morning after prayer, as his father David had instructed him.

When did I cease reading it? Memories began to emerge from long ago...his impatience to get on to the day's tasks and adventures...his annoyance with the tedious reading. He had decided at that time that reading it was irrelevant for such a busy man. After all, he had it memorized by then anyway.

And when was that exactly? He thought hard. *Ah, the morning after Adona gave me the amulet and I promised never to take it off.* The pendant still hung from his neck after all these years.

Solomon lifted the medallion with his right hand and slowly removed it for the first time.

At once, a light blazed on the far wall of his chamber and words written in gold appeared as though engraved there long ago. "The words of the scroll!" the frightened liege exclaimed.

Emblazoned on the alabaster wall were the sacred words:

The king, moreover, must not acquire great numbers of horses for himself or make the people return to

Egypt to get more of them, for the Lord has told you, "You are not to go back that way again." He must not take many wives, or his heart will be led astray. He must not accumulate large amounts of silver and gold. When he takes the throne of his kingdom, he is to write for himself on a scroll a copy of this law, taken from that of the priests, who are Levites. It is to be with him and he is to read it all the days of his life so that he may learn to revere the Lord his God and follow carefully all the words of this law and these decrees and not consider himself better than his brothers and turn from the law to the right or to the left. Then he and his descendants will reign a long time over his kingdom in Israel.[26]

He fell to his face and wept. *Where are You, Promise Giver? Is it too late to find You again?* he cried.

There was no answer.

---

26.   Deuteronomy 17:16-20.

CHAPTER TWENTY

FINDING HIS WAY HOME

H is greatest grief—greater than that which he knew was in store for his kingdom—was that he hadn't felt the Presence of the Promise Giver for some time. In his old age, the child within him cried out for the innocent days of his youth.

His memories of going into the old tabernacle to worship with his father remained vivid. How he identified now with a song his father had composed while in the desert fleeing the mad King Saul!

O God, You are my God,
Earnestly I seek You;
My soul thirsts for You,
My body longs for You,
in a dry and weary land where there is no water.[27]

If only he could find the peace that David always found at the end of each day!

On my bed I remember You;
I think of You through the watches of the night.
Because You are my help,

---

27.   Psalm 63:1.

I sing in the shadow of Your wings.
My soul clings to You;
Your right hand upholds me. [28]

As he sat in a heap on his bedroom floor and thought of the division that would surely come to the kingdom after his death, he could barely endure the images of disaster that could be brought on by a foolish king's reign. And his son appeared to be capable of much foolishness. In that moment, the strains of a desperately melancholy refrain his father had sung when agonizing over the possible outcome of his own mistakes became Solomon's personal lament:

My heart is in anguish within me;
the terrors of death assail me.
Fear and trembling have beset me;
horror has overwhelmed me.
I said, "Oh, that I had the wings of a dove!
I would fly away and be at rest—I would flee far away and
stay in the desert;
I would hurry to my place of shelter,
Far from the tempest and storm." [29]

With this, Solomon could identify. The words gripped his aching heart.

He feared again, as he had before embarking on his voyage to Ethiopia, that he might lose his mind.

And then, as if he could possibly feel any worse, he remembered what it had been like to lead the processions of worshipers to the beautiful Dwelling that he himself had

---

28. Psalm 63:6-8.
29. Psalm 55:4-8.

built. His own shouts of joy and thanksgiving, his own lusty sermons on God's love and righteousness, rang in his ears.

How could I have so lost my way? He began weeping once again.

He went to bed, but slept fitfully.

In the morning as he still lay in bed, he dejectedly put the amulet around his neck once more. It seemed alive on his chest, making him uneasy in his confusion, but he wouldn't remove it. He at least would keep one promise—his promise to Adona. Perhaps faithfulness in this one thing would somehow make up for his unfaithfulness to her as a husband.

The Next Day

Where is Simeon? the king moaned as he pulled himself out of bed and tried to face the day.

When summoned, his dear friend came. Aging and faltering in step, he came. As always, they met in the garden.

Upon entering by his usual route, Simeon was struck by the profusion of weeds among the flowers everywhere he looked. He strained to hear the songs of the exotic birds of the king's menagerie, but only the monotonous tones of a nondescript, gray desert bird that had found its way to the premises was distinguishable. Simeon felt a bit guilty that he didn't miss the peacocks one bit.

This time, the king was pacing the pathway at the far side of the neglected garden—oblivious to all the disarray about him. When he caught sight of his friend, Solomon stopped pacing. A look of relief spread briefly over his countenance.

"I think often of you and your family these days...of the simple joy you have together that money can't buy." He continued with growing intensity, "It seems to me now that the greatest treasure is to work hard with your hands and enjoy life with the wife of your youth, all the days of the life God has given you. This you have done. How wise you have been!"

And then the gloom returned.

"I never managed to make such treasure mine," he whispered.

Then with fear in his eyes and desperation in his voice, he continued, "But beyond that, far worse than that, I have lost my bearings once again, Simeon. I've wandered so far, I can't find my way back to the Promise Giver!" Simeon quickly embraced his distraught friend.

The sorrow in Solomon's voice was fathomless as he spoke of spiritual things. "I have tried to appease a million gods, yet the pleasure of Jehovah cannot be mine. While shrines are planted on every hillside, beside every stream, and in every corner of the palace, the Dwelling that I love is empty to me."

"Do you want to return?" Simeon asked gently as he found his voice again and released the king from his embrace. "He still loves you, Solomon. He promised He would, do you remember?"

They both fell silent. The king was remembering. His labored breathing quieted and a glimmer of hope flickered in his eyes.

Simeon ventured on. "Perhaps you have spent your life doing what you thought the Gift required," he continued gently, "rather than *being* what God enjoyed." After a pause he asked a curious question: "Did you think the Gift of Wisdom obligated you to do what others could not?"

Solomon didn't know what to think of that question. Before he could try to respond, Simeon asked another question in the same gentle way the king loved. "Jehovah's Gift was free, wasn't it?" he probed. Then with a sweeping gesture toward the palace and all that surrounded it, he continued. "Did He *require* all this? Is this what He wanted when He gave you the Gift?"

The king became agitated. "I don't know what He wanted!" he answered, shaking his head from side to side. "If I had known, I'd not be estranged from Him now, would I?" Frustrated, he began pacing again, not waiting for an answer.

Simeon laid his hand on Solomon's shoulder to calm him. The king stopped and drew a deep breath.

"What was the last thing Promise Giver said to you before the heavens became silent?" Simeon asked softly.

The Last Time

"I don't know," the king struggled. "It's been so long," he scratched his chin through his unruly beard and tried to remember.

At that very moment, a lamb bleated loudly in the distance. Soon a host of other lambs followed in what sounded like a plaintive song of resignation. The sound of the lambs bleating triggered Solomon's memory.

"It was after I had taken the story of my love for Deborah, the Song of Songs, to Kephirah for Moshe to hide in the mountains. Eli, Nathaniel, and I were on our way home." His countenance brightened as he remembered that day.

"The hour was three o'clock in the afternoon when our chariot reached the outskirts of Jerusalem, and the ritual of preparing for the evening sacrifice at the Dwelling was underway," he recalled carefully. "At the time, I reflected on all my father had taught me about the need for a sacrifice for our sin and how, someday, Messiah would come

and be the ultimate sacrifice, doing away with the daily ritual of shedding blood. I remember that well..." his eyes had
a faraway look in them.

"I then thought about an incredible vision I had seen
when I was only a boy, before I was ever crowned king."
This piqued Simeon's interest greatly.

"Tell me about it, Solomon, please!" he urged.

The king studied his friend's face for a moment, and
then decided to proceed. He recounted it just as he had
experienced it all those years ago...the crossed beams in the
sky, the simple Shepherd who willingly allowed Himself to
be brutally slain upon them as evil spears were thrown by
unseen hands, the eyes of the Lamb, the massive throne,
and the heart of the King who then sat upon it—the Shepherd who had mysteriously become King.

All Simeon could do was wonder at this miracle and
hope that he might live long enough to see it for himself.
They both drew deep breaths and decided to finish the rest
of their visit comfortably sitting on a nearby bench. After
brushing dead leaves and sand from it, they sat and
resumed their amazing discussion.

The king continued, "At the time, after remembering
the vision as I rode back into Jerusalem, I begged Promise
Giver to help me understand it all."

"Then what happened?" Simeon prompted.

"Immediately, I felt an infinite, unseen arm of love
drawing me close. It was the warmest, safest sensation I
had felt since my father died," he exclaimed and then
added, "No woman can make a man feel so loved and safe."
He paused again, as though still processing this concept.

"And then He spoke." In a quivering voice, Solomon
repeated what Promise Giver had spoken into his heart that
day. *"Someday, when you have faced the demons within and*

refused them the right to make you suffer, you will under-
stand. When your own way is spent, the pain will end."

Simeon again prompted him. "Then what happened?"

The king slowly shook his head in disbelief. "I actually shook it off and sought the arms of one of my wives," he
admitted in shame.

His friend touched his arm comfortingly. "Solomon,
what would you say to Him if you were sure He was listening right now?" he ventured to ask.

"I don't think He wants to hear from me at this late
date," the king mumbled sorrowfully.

Just then, Simeon spotted the Egyptian amulet that
hung from the king's neck. Usually discreetly hidden
beneath his tunic, this morning, it had slipped out and
caught Simeon's eye.

"What's that?" he asked curiously, pointing to the
pendant.

Looking down at it, the king replied absently, "Just a
gift Adona gave me years ago."

"You know," Simeon continued as he studied the
image of Pharaoh and the serpent that stood out in relief on
its surface, "these are considered a powerful charm among
those who worship the gods of Egypt." Then with sudden
alarm, he exclaimed, "This represents everything Jehovah
delivered us from when Moses led our ancestors out of that
pagan country! You've slowly joined forces with the enemy
of our nation and our souls!" Simeon jumped to his feet
and took an involuntary step back and away from the king
as this realization dawned on him. He was horrified.

Then instinctively, like a warrior doing battle for his
life, the gentle, retiring Simeon acted out of character. He
lunged forward, grabbed the pendant, and boldly challenged

the king. "Rid yourself of this curse! Rid this nation of the idolatry that has gripped it by freeing yourself first!"

Solomon responded with the first ounce of freedom he had tasted in a long, long time. He tore the chain from his neck and threw the amulet as far as he could and with all the strength he could muster! It smashed against the wall of the garden and shattered—a very strange thing indeed for a solid gold piece to do!

"I want His Presence more than life itself!" he shouted for all the world to hear. "Jehovah alone is God; He alone made Heaven and earth; He alone can deliver His people! The Messiah will come! Fear Him, O Israel, and keep His commandments for this is the whole duty of man!"

The heavens opened and Promise Giver spoke into his spirit, *You have now spoken the truth, My son. Know this: All the wisdom of the Gift is contained in your simple proclamation.* Solomon's heart pounded and tears filled His eyes at hearing the Voice once again. *And know this as well: My love has never lessened for you, nor have I ever been far from you. But there was so much sin between you and Me, you couldn't hear My voice. The king sobbed in shame.*

Then gently, the Voice continued. *All the Gift was meant to accomplish was to help you lead the people in obedience and holiness so that you would all be blessed. You wasted your gift on things that didn't matter. If you had simply taken Me seriously and pursued Me with all your heart, I would have blessed you with everything wonderful anyway. Do you understand?* Promise Giver queried the broken king.

"I understand that I have been a fool and that guilt has been lifted with my confession," he acknowledged with relief. "I understand that there is no point to life without

Your blessing, no hope for peace apart from You, no protection against insanity but in Your Presence!" the king further confessed.

As Simeon stood dumbfounded—watching and hearing the king, but seeing and hearing no one else—Promise Giver continued instructing Solomon.

Speak to your son, Solomon. Use what little time you have left to prepare him for the battle ahead. That is all you can do. I will do the rest.

"What about the Promise?" the king asked.

It is enough for you to know that He will come through the remnant of Israel that will prove itself faithful in the years to come. Messiah will come, and someday in Heaven, you will see Him face to face.

The voice fell silent, but the Presence wrapped the old king as in a soft blanket. Seeing that Solomon needed to be alone with Promise Giver, Simeon slipped away unnoticed and returned home. His job was done.

A New Start

Weak in body—but stronger in spirit than he had been since childhood—Solomon made his way back to his chambers sometime later as the sun dropped behind the hills to the west.

In the morning, he pulled out of his desk a beautiful piece of parchment that he had been saving for something special. He hadn't penned any proverbs for a very long time. This day, he etched these words:

> *The king's heart is in the hand of the Lord;*
> *He directs it like a watercourse wherever He pleases.*
> *All a man's ways seem right to him,*
> *but the Lord weighs the heart.*

A man who strays from the path of understanding
comes to rest in the company of the dead.
He who pursues righteousness and love
Finds life, prosperity and honor.
There is no wisdom, no insight, no plan
that can succeed against the Lord.
The horse is made ready for the day of battle,
but victory rests with the Lord.[30]

In the abyss, Traeh's long, horny neck twisted and turned, as he tried to see what the king was writing. But he could not. His scaly sides heaved with anger as tongues of flame flashed from the grotesque chasm behind his decaying teeth.

He despised Promise Giver; he despised the power of His love against which his own hate too often failed.

With his long bony tail lashing from side to side, set in motion by the fury that gripped him and wouldn't let him go, he vowed: "I will not concede defeat! It's not over yet!"

But then he heard the sound he hated most. Carried on the breath of God from the heavens far beyond the universe came a song...the song the angels sang in times of victory.

Traeh spread his great, bony wings and caught another wind, the breath of hell that rose from the world of the damned. Upon that wind he soared and circled, beating his wings in fury as he spewed fire down upon the already scorched and barren sod of hell.

---

30.   Proverbs 21:1-2, 16, 21, 30-31.

CHAPTER TWENTY-ONE

TRUTH REVEALED

Solomon's health was failing fast. While his spirit was at rest, his body struggled through each new day.

His son, Rehoboam, spent most of his free time with a cadre of young men who had been raised on the benefits of the privileged class. Their fathers were either military commanders or overseers of the pleasure cities where the boys wasted their nights and escaped responsibility.

"He's a good boy at heart," Solomon spoke weakly to Aaron, his most trusted counselor, now that Barak was dead and gone.

"Of course, my king. But he knows too little of suffering and has no vision for leadership." He lowered his voice and leaned forward toward the king who was reclining on a couch in the judgment hall, resting from the morning at court. "I fear he can too easily be manipulated by self-serving confidantes."

The old king sighed and turned his head away, his eyes searching the frescoes on the wall at the foot of his couch.

Remembering Jehovah's admonition to him to speak with his son, and now prompted by Aaron, Solomon voiced his intention. "I'll talk with him today."

Confessions

That night, after receiving the command from Solomon to meet with him in the palace garden before sunset,

Rehoboam sought his father out. The garden was again immaculately kept and the birds had returned. The king's newly gained peace of mind and peace with God had restored order to all he touched.

The two men met face to face and Solomon led the way to a newly created alcove. In the center of the stone patio was a cleverly designed fountain from which splashed clear, sparkling water, whose very sound refreshed all who came near. Arranged congenially around it were three ornately decorated bronze benches with velvet cushions lining the seats and softening the backs.

The king motioned to his son to take a seat on one of them. He then sat upon an adjacent bench where he could monitor his son's expressions.

"How have you been Rehoboam?" he began awkwardly. "I haven't seen much of you lately," he added without judgment.

"Oh," the boy answered with a quick smile, "I'm fine. All my needs have been taken care of, thank you."

"Every need but that of time with me," the king responded regretfully. "I'm sorry I have been such a poor father and friend to you. I have spent a lifetime being busy over all the wrong things, I fear."

The boy shifted uneasily on the bench. He wasn't accustomed to such candor from his famous father.

"Will you please forgive me, Son?" Solomon asked sincerely.

Rehoboam's face reddened at such a request. He managed a reply. "Of course, Father." He nervously studied the embroidery along the hem of his robe and hoped the subject would soon change.

Solomon got the unspoken message and accommodated his son. "I called you here for that reason and to speak of the future. I know my behavior in recent years has betrayed all I taught you as a child, but I beg you not to repeat my mistakes!"

He drew a deep breath and continued. "Don't trust in riches or power; trust in the Lord with all your heart." He looked into his son's eyes, only to see confusion. But he pressed on. "Don't pursue the idols that I have foolishly allowed into our nation. Instead, call on the name of the Lord and He will direct your paths and make your way straight."

Rehoboam looked at his father with mixed emotions now. He hungered for his instructions, but wondered if it was too little too late. Regardless, he began drinking in every word whether he understood it or not.

"And, Son," the king went on, his voice gaining strength and resonating with conviction, "above all else, guard your heart, for it is the wellspring of your whole life." With deep sadness, he confessed, "This is the advice your grandfather gave me when I was your age, but I was too foolish to heed it." With passion, he warned, "Take one woman of your people to be your wife and then drink only of her love all the days of your life." Looking deep into Rehoboam's eyes he further warned, "Don't be unfaithful to her!"

At this, Rehoboam looked at him in wonderment. *My father—who has captured the hearts of a thousand women and is the envy of all my friends who seek women nightly—is telling me to focus on just one woman! I don't believe this!*

Reading his son's thoughts, Solomon concluded his advice with deep sincerity, "May you be blessed with many children and may you rejoice in the wife of your youth." And then the inevitable caution: "For a man's ways are in full view of the Lord and He examines every deed."

Slowly, enunciating every word, Solomon told his son, "I have been a fool, but you don't need to be."

Rehoboam's face was flushed with self-consciousness and he again wished his father would change the subject.

Solomon did. "And now, for the days ahead..." *Ah,* thought Rehoboam excitedly, *now for talk of power and politics!*

A servant suddenly appeared with wine, fruit, and cheese for their refreshment. Over an interval of light conversation, they ate and drank, but Solomon was anxious to get back to instructing his son.

"Choose your counselors well, my boy," he resumed when the trays had been removed by the servant and they were alone again. "They can make you or break you. Furthermore, pride breeds quarrels, but wisdom is found in those who take advice...advice from those trained well by experience," the king warned. "My trusted advisors will be at your disposal. Listen to them, Son. They will know what to do to set things right in the land." Then the old king's voice fell as he sadly admitted, "I wish I had listened to them myself."

The youth couldn't imagine what wisdom those old codgers could have for his generation. *When I become king, I will decide for myself who should or shouldn't advise me! he secretly resolved. I will humor the old man now to avoid more of these awkward sessions,* he concluded.

The king, content that he had said all he'd intended and knowing that Promise Giver had said He would do the rest, drew the meeting to a close.

As they rose to go, Solomon gripped his son's arm. "If you remember nothing else of what I have said today, Son, remember this: Fear God and keep His commandments, for this is the sum total of what God asks of us. It's that simple.

All else of joy and fulfillment for anyone, king or peasant, grows out of obedience to that truth."

Rehoboam quickly left ahead of his father, anxious to rejoin his friends. The old man exited slowly, planning the next difficult conversation as he went. He was on his way to speak with Adona.

More Amends

He found her in her private chambers in the Queen's Palace, the Forest of Lebanon. This suite was her solace, the only part of the palace she had not been forced to share with most of Solomon's subsequent wives. Here she spent her days in retirement, embroidering and dreaming of Egypt and home.

The servant announced the king's presence. He respectfully waited at the doorway, even though he could have entered at will. He had not summoned her or gone to her for a long, long time.

"Adona, may I speak with you?" he softly inquired.

Startled, she dropped her needle, and it fell silently to the floor, landing on an exquisite Persian rug. She stood slowly to her feet and bowed slightly, still holding her embroidery in one hand.

Solomon entered and asked her to please sit again. A servant took his cue and drew another deeply tufted divan near her and eased the old king onto it.

He began rather abruptly, deciding to get right to the point. "I have not been a good husband to you, nor even a good friend." He faltered, hoping for some encouragement from her to continue. There was nothing but a weary look in her eyes as she scanned his visage and form. His tunic, open at the neck, caught her attention. Something was different.

She instantly stiffened. The amulet was missing! That alone had remained their point of connection through the years, reminding them of what they had in common. Now it was gone.

"Where is it?" she demanded.

Knowing at once by her gaze at his chest and throat that the issue was the pendant and his promise to her, the king answered cautiously, "I removed it."

"And where is it now?" she pressed on, her anger mounting.

He gulped. "I smashed it."

"You *what*?" she rose, her arm outstretched and her finger pointing accusingly at Solomon. "You promised you would wear that forever! How could you break such a sacred promise—the only one I ever asked of you?" she shouted.

"Making that promise broke one I had made to Jehovah long before that," he answered simply, tired of clever replies. "In order to restore the first promise, I had to break the latter."

Throwing her embroidery work at him, she seethed, "I never want to see your face again." Her voice was low and venomous, reminding him of the serpent that had festooned the amulet. "Get out of here with your Jehovah, you promise breaker!"

He rose to leave. It had not gone as he had hoped. But in relief that the encounter was over, he left as quickly as he could. However, his heart was full of sorrow that he had used her life as he had. It had not been right.

At the threshold of the room, he called back barely loudly enough for her to hear, "I'm sorry, Adona, for everything. It was not your fault, only mine."

Increasing Freedom

Paradoxically, with the sorrow that deepened as he realized how his pursuit of pleasure had often cost others pain, came a new measure of freedom as truth began to flow from his lips once again. It had been a long time. Life was beginning to right itself as he sought the heart of the God who had made him nearly sixty years ago.

He wrote with new determination, but his writing was laced with melancholy. It was as if he were making the journey to spiritual childhood with the heart of an old man. He had changed. He could never again be a little boy at his father's knee, fascinated with life and in love with the world.

The wisdom he had thought he had was gone. A quiet awareness of the majesty of God, the holiness of His Presence, and the overwhelming task of keeping a nation with its face in the right direction had replaced it.

Perhaps I could begin as king again, he mused as he sat by his open window, his elbow on the sill and his bearded cheek resting upon his open hand. But he knew it was too late. He could only pray that his nation would survive the spiritual damage he had done during the latter part of his reign.

His pulse quickened at the thought. *The Messiah—the Promise—will come. Promise Giver said so Himself. We surely can remain a people until then and provide Him with the throne He should have!* An excitement rose in the old king's heart. He remembered the throne he had seen in his vision—magnificent and embedded with beautiful gems. He remembered the eyes of the King...and was drawn up short. *Will the throne even matter to this King when He comes?* He wondered.

Solomon also wondered why it had ever mattered so much in his own life....

The Last Night

The monarch who had penned a thousand proverbs didn't write anything that night. He who had solved mysterious riddles, astounded others with his wise judgments, named hundreds of species of plant life, and dictated building plans for the most magnificent structures ever conceived in Israel, found that, for the first time, he had nothing more to say.

The old dreamer simply went to sleep that night, cradled in the arms of Jehovah.

And his dreams were sweet. It was as though Jehovah carried him out of his bed and gently placed him down on the ground below the window of his childhood room in his father's old palace. It seemed quite natural for it to happen that way. But then the sounds of a celebration caught his ears and he began walking quickly down the street in the direction of the cheering.

Crowds were gathering to the left just inside the city's main gate and the air was charged with festivity.

"He's coming! The King is coming!" Men, women with babies in their arms, and children all passed the news, chattering at once, as they rushed toward the crowd that was growing rapidly. As they ran, they were tearing palm branches from the trees and waving them wildly in the air!

"Hosanna to the King! Blessed is He who comes in the name of the Lord!" the shouts rang.

And then He appeared.

A plain man in a simple, nondescript robe gathered at the waist by a worn leather belt, rode astride a young donkey. His sandaled feet, dusty and callused from endless miles of travel on foot, hung nearly to the ground from the sides of the small animal. His face and hands were bronzed from the sun; His hair and beard framed His features in soft brown tones. And Solomon wasn't surprised.

As this simple man neared the spot where he now stood, the stranger's eyes probed Solomon's for an instant.

But in that instant, the "knowing" of an old man who had finally learned how to look into eternity settled upon the earthly king.

This was the King of the crossed beams who alone deserved to sit upon the golden throne. Their eyes locked for an instant in understanding. And then the dream was gone. The old man slept on peacefully.

Regardless of what was to come on earth, his heart would claim Heaven.

Sometime near midnight, the king stirred peacefully in his bed and whispered, "My heart is Yours, Promise Giver."

I know, Son, I know.

EPILOGUE

❦

And, so, the old king died—wise at last. Silently, he slipped out of the constraints of earth and into the freedom of Heaven.

In the cosmic gulf between Heaven and hell, the ponderous iron scales emerged once again—empty this time, the battle over, the heart of the once-sleeping baby boy held safely in the arms of his Lord. But it was a battle too nearly lost, too full of heartache.

Meanwhile, Traeh paced the bowels of hell, his razor-sharp tail swinging viciously from side to side and his bony claws ripping into the lifeless clay sod of the abyss. Every sinew in his body quivered with resentment.

"Don't celebrate too soon, Promise Giver," snarled the ancient Dark Dragon as he spat venom into the murky air that surrounded him. "These puny victories of Yours will mean nothing when I destroy the Promise!" Summoning all the hate he had sown since the world was born, the beast bellowed, "Mark my words: I will see Your Messiah in hell before I'm through!"

With his jagged jaws opened wide, Traeh let out a blood-curdling roar, the flames from his foul breath scorching the stars that dotted the heavens above. His ugly head cocked to one side, he strained to hear a response from Heaven. All was silent.

The sky turned dark as time moved on...
and earth waited for the Promise.

Destiny Image Fiction
by Joyce Strong

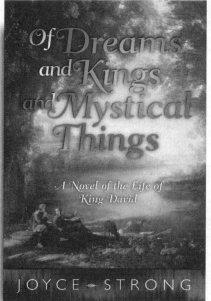

OF DREAMS AND KINGS AND MYSTICAL THINGS

This book weaves an exciting prophetic drama of King David and what the shape and fabric of his divine encounters might have been. His love for his Lord and his devotion and desire are magnified in the pages of this book. You will wish you were David as you read of the powerful relationship he experienced with his Lord. But read on—you will quickly discover that this love experience can be yours as well.

ISBN: 0-7684-3044-5

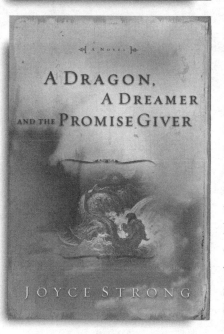

A DRAGON, A DREAMER, AND THE PROMISE GIVER

King Solomon, son of the legendary David, is a paradox of epic proportions—a poet by night, and a politician by day. Lonely and disillusioned, he must choose his fate. Will Solomon's bitterness cost him his soul? Does the Dark Dragon win his heart in the end? Laced with vivid imagery and haunted by lost love, this tale takes us on a fascinating journey back in time to the ancient land of Israel, nearly a thousand years before Christ.

ISBN: 0-7684-2182-9

Available at your local Christian bookstore.

Additional copies of this book and other book titles from DESTINY IMAGE are available at your local bookstore.

For a complete list of our titles, visit us at www.destinyimage.com Send a request for a catalog to:

Destiny Image® Publishers, Inc.
P.O. Box 310
Shippensburg, PA 17257-0310

"Speaking to the Purposes of God for This Generation and for the Generations to Come"